Alma,

Best wishes

Lauri Anderson

Suomi College, 1993

HUNTING HEMINGWAY'S TROUT

HUNTING HEMINGWAY'S TROUT

Stories

LAURI ANDERSON

ATHENEUM
NEW YORK 1990
COLLIER MACMILLAN CANADA • TORONTO

MAXWELL MACMILLAN INTERNATIONAL
NEW YORK • OXFORD • SINGAPORE • SYDNEY

Atheneum
Macmillan Publishing Company
866 Third Avenue, New York, N.Y. 10022

Collier Macmillan Canada, Inc.
1200 Eglinton Avenue East, Suite 200
Don Mills, Ontario M3C 3N1

Library of Congress Cataloging-in-Publication Data
Anderson, Lauri.
    Hunting Hemingway's trout : stories / Lauri Anderson.
        p.   cm.
    ISBN 0-689-12103-2
    I. Title.
PS3551.N37444H8   1990
813'.54—dc20   90-37406   CIP

Macmillan books are available at special discounts for bulk purchases for sales promotions, premiums, fund-raising, or educational use. For details, contact:

Special Sales Director
Macmillan Publishing Company
866 Third Avenue
New York, N.Y. 10022

10 9 8 7 6 5 4 3 2 1

Printed in the United States of America

FOR CHARLOTTE
AND ERIC

HUNTING HEMINGWAY'S TROUT

PICTURES

The picture is an enlargement of an old photo that my mother gave my younger brother Stuart when Stuart last made a rare visit from California to the homeplace in northern Maine.

In the picture my father is a young man—younger than I am now—posturing with a dead bear. My muscular father fills the right half of the picture. He has one knee on the ground against the left rear haunch of the bear while the other supports his left forearm. The right forearm rests on the dead bear's forehead.

The dead bear dominates the lower half of the picture. His front shoulders and head seem to be curled against my father's knee and forearm as if the bear were an overgrown pup asking to be rubbed. In reality a wooden stake supports the bear's forebody. One point of the stake is driven into the ground. The other is driven into the bear's neck.

The background brings faint memories. It's the barn at my grandfather's farm—the barn that fell down over thirty years ago. Before it fell, Uncle Leon threw open cans of red paint at it, decorating the weathered boards with huge red circles that ran toward the ground.

I

*   *   *

The picture pulls me deep into the past, into a world that preceded my existence. That distant world is Finnish. My grandparents speak only Finnish. Somewhere outside the closed narrow box of the photo, Matti and Louise converse in their incomprehensible language. The words are unknown to me. So is the subject matter. My grandparents speak of the farm—of working with horses, of drying hay, of canning, of gardening, of milking, of berrying. They have strange ways of doing things. They make yogurt of the milk. Americans of my generation do not make yogurt. My grandparents slaughter their own animals and salt the meat. Americans of my generation do not salt meat; they can get thick steaks daily at the supermarket. My father knows how to do these things. He grew up on that Finnish farm and can create his own hog's headcheese, blood sausage, flatbread. He traps bear and coon and shoots deer and rabbit. My father makes gloves and moccasins from the deerskin and a rug from the bearskin. He eats the meat. My father will eat anything at least once.

Did my Finnish-hating mother take the picture? I have difficulty imagining her as a visitor at the Finnish grandparents' farm. My mother is DAR. Her roots and the country's roots are the same. Long before the Revolution some unknown ancestor crossed the Atlantic to the British colonies in the New World. One of them founded the town of Lee, Maine, before Maine existed as a state.

My mother's family has always known with absolute certainty that they are right. In all things. My mother knows this. She knows that Finnishness must therefore be wrong because it is not part of the rightness of old New England.

But my father is a very attractive man. My mother the photographer will marry him. Maybe has married him. It's her great opportunity. He's handsome, strong, thirty, terribly shy, has his own business. She's done with school, has begun to teach, is no one's idea of beauty. She has a soft round body as lumpy and bumpy and oddly shaped as an old potato. Her eyes are bulbous, her hair frizzy. In addition she has a violent temper, prejudiced judgment, and a long list of phobias. Frightened of much of life, she will blame these fears on my father. He will become, until he dies, the eternal scapegoat, the root of all bumps in the night.

Why will he marry her? Is it her berry pies? She can cook. Surely that is not enough. He shouldn't do it. In the picture he looks proud and happy. He has shot a bear and had his picture taken.

I want to warn him. I stare at his picture, implore him not to do it—not to conceive five children in the womb of old New England.

Years later, when I am yet a tiny child, he will give his in-laws the money to buy a farm. They will never repay him. He will bring the New Englanders sides of beef and whole pigs and lambs. He will package the meat for them—slice the tenderloin into steaks, saw the ribs for barbecues. They will never acknowledge his gifts, his talents. They are inside a wall two hundred years old, inside a wall erected long before his Finnishness ever existed in their geography. My mother is inside the wall. My father is not.

Later still we children—locked out from our father's world by our mother—will choose to reject our mother's world. We will stand alone in a wilderness—not Finnish and not old New England. What are we? We are nothing. We are America.

*   *   *

Our father will drive too fast. He will carry my mother over a woodpile. That will be the first accident. In the second he will take her into a telephone pole. She will shatter her leg. They will insert metal screws and plates. The trauma will bring on diabetes. The diabetes will eat her legs and take away her sight. She will become a sort of vegetable—physically helpless but her keen mind still intact.

My father will die of a stroke. But in the picture he is intensely alive. All the little deaths lie ahead. I lie ahead. Detour, father, detour!

My mother sits helplessly and hopelessly in a nursing home in old New England. She cannot see the picture of my handsome young father-to-be. She has no eyes. Diabetes. The picture is in Michigan's Upper Peninsula in my living room on the piano. The father in the picture is surrounded by Finnishness. In every direction the street signs are in Finnish. The population is Finnish. The names of surrounding towns—Tapiola, Toivola, Paavola—are Finnish. Even the bread we eat—rieska—is Finnish. The college where I teach is Finnish.

Father, you've come home.

And I?

Still nothing. America.

I sit in my living room in a rocker that faces my father's picture. Piled beside me on the floor are a half dozen biographies of Ernest Hemingway. Each invents a different Ernest. I pick up the top one and open to the family pictures inserted between pages 150 and 151.

There are two pictures of young Dr. Hemingway alone, Ernest's father. In each the doctor sits stiffly, his face impassive and, except for the eyes, emptied of life. In a third picture the family poses formally on a beach as if they were in a Chicago salon. Mrs. Grace Hall Hemingway dominates the picture. She is in the foreground wearing a sort of sailor suit with broad bright trim and a wide collar. A sailor hat is perched at an angle on her head. She wears high laced boots. She smiles. She holds an unsmiling Ernest. He is perhaps three.

The doctor sits behind her, his face a dark blotch of shadow without features. Little daughter Marcelline sits forward on the doctor's knee. Her face gathers light. She doesn't smile.

In front of the doctor the reel end of a fishing rod sits on the earth. The handle has been wrapped with friction tape for better grip, but the doctor clutches awkwardly at the rod with his thumb. The rest of his hand supports Marcelline.

In the fourth picture the doctor sits again in the background. This time only the right side of his impassive face is in shadow. He wears a dark suit that blends without distinction into the equally dark background.

The foreground is a row of Hemingways. On the doctor's right knee sits Ursula in a bright frilly outfit chosen by her mother. On the doctor's left knee sits Ernest, also in a bright frilly outfit. Ernest is perhaps four. Neither he nor Ursula smiles. The doctor's hands encircle their waists.

Beside Ernest (not beside her husband) sits Mrs. Grace Hall Hemingway. Her face gathers light. She smiles. Her hair is an elaborate coiffure dominated by a large bow tipped sharply toward her right ear. Her clothes are bright and lacy. Lace encircles her neck and flows to her waist. She looks large.

The doctor looks small.

Beside Mrs. Grace Hall Hemingway is Marcelline. She too wears a frilly outfit and a bow that matches her mother's, including the angle. Marcelline, however, does not smile.

These are portraits of the Hemingway family.

I look in the book at the portraits of Dr. Hemingway. I look across my living room at the portrait of my father. Ernest would have admired my father if the two had met. They were of comparable age, Ernest older by ten years. Ernest admired any man like my father who could make his own way—who could hunt, fish, camp, canoe. Ernest's father could also do all of these things and did them often. Until he married. After that every year diminished his life as an outdoorsman.

Mrs. Grace Hall Hemingway wanted more than anything to be an opera star. She was extremely proud of her voice, as was my mother of hers. Like my mother, she had weak eyes. The weak eyes could not take stage lighting. Maybe her voice wasn't quite good enough either. She fell back on marriage to the doctor. But she designed their home to include a thirty-foot-long music room with fifteen-foot-high walls. Like my mother, she involved herself in the Congregational church choir, women's clubs, and fine arts events. When their position in the church was threatened by those they considered upstarts, both women changed churches.

The doctor doctored. He also hired a cook because his wife did not cook. He hired a maid because his wife did not do housework. He hired a mother's aid because Grace's time with the children was limited. The doctor also fired these people when his wife found them inadequate. Until replacements could be found, the doctor cooked and cleaned up. He made very good berry pies. He brought his wife breakfast in bed.

Mrs. Grace Hall Hemingway extolled her ancestry to her children. She disdained the Hemingways. She named all of her children after their maternal relatives. She traced her ancestry to old New England—to John Hancock and to the Revolutionary spirit.

Mrs. Grace Hall Hemingway kept a companion for years—a live-in friend and student who adored Grace. The doctor eventually drove the companion out of the house. One can only guess why.

The doctor had a cottage in Michigan. Every summer the family went there. At first the doctor went too. Then he couldn't find the time. He stopped hunting and fishing and collecting Indian curios. His wife threw the curios away.

Mrs. Grace Hall Hemingway hated the cottage in Michigan because there was no maid, no cook, no mother's aid. She much preferred Oak Park and nearby Chicago. Eventually she built her own cottage across the lake from the family cottage.

Mrs. Grace Hall Hemingway's son would write many stories about Michigan. About Oak Park he would write nothing.

In 1928 at age fifty-seven Dr. Hemingway committed suicide. Later his famous son Ernest and two other children (Ursula and Leicester) would follow his example. Possibly Marcelline too.

Mrs. Grace Hall Hemingway lived to a ripe old age.

*   *   *

I wonder if Hemingway looked at his father's pictures just as I have done. I wonder if he saw what I saw. Certainly he saw his father as a victim of marriage. That view comes out in his stories.

He must have seen himself as such a victim sometimes too. He changed wives four times.

Maybe both men should have detoured.

Father, do not do it! Dr. Hemingway, do not do it!

Ernest, we need to console each other. But you died of a self-inflicted gunshot wound in Ketchum, Idaho, a long time ago.

And I? Alone. America.

A BIT ABOUT HEMINGWAY

Ernest Hemingway was born in the affluent Chicago suburb of Oak Park on July 21, 1899. A smug, self-important Republican enclave, Oak Park was a dry town of strict morality and little passion. Ernest had an older sister, three younger sisters, and a brother fifteen years younger than he. Ernest attended Oak Park High School. Some of his neighbors were Frank Lloyd Wright and Edgar Rice Burroughs.

Although he never wrote even a paragraph about Oak Park, Ernest did name the cowardly Francis Macomber after a local insurance agent who gave a prize for the best eighth-grade essay on the importance of life insurance.

Ernest spent summers until he was twenty-one at the family cottage on Walloon Lake near Petoskey, Michigan. There he learned to love the outdoors, to hunt, to fish. He used Michigan as the setting for ten stories, for sections of two additional stories, and for a short novel.

Later Ernest either lived in, worked in, or traveled in Kansas City, Key West, Wyoming, Montana, Idaho, New York, St. Louis, Arkansas, Paris, southern France, Germany, England,

Switzerland, Italy, Spain, Turkey, Greece, China, British East Africa, Suez. This list is not inclusive.

Ernest spoke Spanish, Italian, French, a little Swahili, and Hollywood pidgin Indian.

Ernest died of a self-inflicted gunshot to the head in Ketchum, Idaho, in 1961.

HUNTING HEMINGWAY'S TROUT

Cousin Toivo and I bucked the empty truck along a two-track logging road that one of the Vainio boys had bulldozed out of the forest in late spring. In the past month Toivo had selected the largest birch trees for cutting. As he had dropped them I had dragged them by tractor to the roadside. At the end of each day Toivo had cut the logs into four-foot sections suitable for pulp, which I had piled along the road. Now we were loading the truck in sticky hot July but at least the heat kept most of the blackflies swarming down in the coolness of the swamp.

Toivo used a clear patch in the forest to turn around and then parked the truck beside our twenty-cord woodpile.

We were in our work togs—jeans stained and stiffened from tree sap, flannel shirts ragged at the elbows, baseball caps sweat-blackened at the bands, leather swampers saturated with bear grease. Our faces were streaked with mosquito dope and dirt. As Cousin Toivo often said, "If you look ugly, you feel ugly, and in this kind of work a man ought to be ugly."

Both of us were feeling particularly ugly that day because we had loaded and unloaded the truck by hand three times a day for ten consecutive days. I knew that was about to change, though, because Toivo had bought a pack of Stroh's on our return from the mill yard for this final load.

The truck radio was playing a song about driving daddy into an early grave, then another about the back door always being open. Toivo placed two open cans of Stroh's on the truck hood and we commenced. First the two of us wrestled upright the thickest butt ends and leaned these against the empty truck bed. Then Toivo climbed onto the bed, his body bent and his birch hook ready. From the ground I hooked the base of a log and heaved. Toivo caught the top end and pulled. Straining together we somehow managed to lift and twist the huge logs—most with girths three or four times greater than our waists—onto the bed, our bulging back muscles as taut as bowstrings. As soon as we had covered the bed with these monsters, Toivo climbed down and joined me at the front bumper where we sat in exhausted silence and drank the Stroh's.

This was the third straight summer I had worked in the woods with Cousin Toivo, and God how I hated it! The pay wasn't much either. However, it saved me from looking for another job and it made my Finnish father happy. Toivo was the difficult child of Aunt Ellen's first marriage. Toivo and I were the same age, but while I had spent my childhood in my room reading books and staying out of trouble, Toivo was out somewhere smashing up a half dozen bikes, accidentally stepping on dozens of nails, picking frequent fights with whoever was bigger and stronger, and unintentionally setting several brushfires while smoking in someone's back field. Toivo was book dumb and undisciplined, but I admired his practicality and his *sisu*—his bulldog courage.

After the beer break, we both worked from the ground. We took opposite sides with heavier logs, spaced our legs for maximum leverage, swung our hooks into the wood and, at Toivo's count of three, heaved upward and outward together. Occasionally a log missed its place in the growing load and slammed back to earth, gouging a deep hole. We'd leap back, curse, leap forward, slam in our hooks anew, and once again heave against our straining back muscles. I could feel the bones in my spine about to snap at the moment we released each log and sent it bedward.

"It's a good thing you're not like other loggers," I said, streams of sweat stinging my eyes. "They all have jammers to load their trucks. They miss out on the real pleasure that comes from loading by hand—the torn back muscles, the sore leg and arm muscles, the sweat, the sawdust in the eyes, the dirt and grime."

"I don't need a jammer," said Toivo. "All that fancy machinery for hoisting a log is expensive and I've got a dumb college student who's cheap."

As the pile grew, it became impossible from the ground to fit each new log snugly against its neighbors. Cousin Toivo climbed onto the load and, as I tossed logs skyward, he caught each deftly with his hook, scrambled aside, and guided it in flight to its proper spot. As the load grew to completion, Toivo was twelve feet in the air and doing a sort of clumsy dance since footing was notoriously unstable among the smaller logs that filled out the top. These thin final logs felt like matchsticks compared to the monsters that formed the base. Now I chose one of the smallest logs, stepped several paces back from the truck, rushed forward and, as if throwing a fat javelin from my knees, propelled the log with maximum velocity toward Toivo. Somehow at the last moment he pirouetted out of the way, caught with his hook the weighty missile in flight, and guided it to its chosen place. The next log failed to reach the top, but Toivo's hook caught it anyway. He let go before the weight of the log could yank him off the truck, but he lost his balance and fell awkwardly to his knees, crunching one against a knot. I leaped back as Toivo's falling hook snapped loose and narrowly missed my face. The point buried itself three inches into the hard-packed earth between my spraddled legs.

"Are you all right?" I asked as I retrieved the errant hook and tossed it back onto the load within easy reach of Toivo. Toivo rose slowly and tested his bruised knee against his own weight. He unsheathed the gutting knife he always carried on his belt and lopped off the offending knot. Then he swore loudly, took up his hook, and motioned that we should continue.

In Gaylord, Michigan, in July the sun doesn't set until after nine, so we still had a few minutes of daylight remaining when we completed the loading. As the air cooled the flies rose in a black cloud off the swamp and headed our way. We could hear the approach. It sounded like a hundred chain saws all roaring at once. Toivo and I retreated to the truck cab just before the swarm turned the air into a seething mass. All around us the forest began to waver and shimmer as if we were undersea. Part of the cloud settled an inch deep onto the warmth of the hood. Another part coated the windshield with an insect curtain so opaque that we had to use the wipers in order to see the road.

We each drank two more Stroh's before Toivo turned the ignition and drove for home. By then it was dark and the insect swarm had spread itself throughout the forest. "When they first come out, they'd eat a man right to the bone in minutes," said Toivo matter-of-factly. "I've seen it before. They caught one of my dogs last year and drained him of blood. There were flies covering every inch—his eyes, nostrils, the inside of his ears. I had to shoot him."

"A good thing we can hear them coming," I said.

"And the worst days are coming," said Toivo. "These recent rains started a new cycle. Another batch of flies will be hatching in the next couple of days."

I knew from the tone of his voice that Toivo had just found the excuse he needed to take a day off. Tomorrow we'd leave the forest to the blackflies while we sought pleasures elsewhere.

"You ever read Hemingway?" said Cousin Toivo as we turned from the two-track onto a gravel road that would lead to the paved road that would take us home.

"Sure," I replied. "I've read lots of his stuff. I enjoy his writing a lot." I was a graduate student in English at the state university and I'd taken several American literature courses in which we studied Hemingway. I worked with my cousin only during summer vacation, thank God, because three months at a time was all I could take of life as a logger. Felling trees wasn't too bad but Cousin Toivo insisted on doing that himself. He said I was too educated to be trusted with a chain saw. I peeled when we were cutting softwood, and always I loaded and unloaded the truck. Always I worried that I would snap my back and instantly become a cripple for the rest of my life. That had happened with my father. Years ago he had bent over while standing on top of a load of maple. That's all he did—just bent over. It took two guys to get him off the load. He couldn't move. He couldn't even sit in the cab when they finally got him down. He rode to the hospital still bent like an old clothespin. I guess he rested his forehead on the dash and his knuckles on the floorboard. After that he couldn't do much of anything, so he clerked in a shoe store. Permanently bent like that, he could put shoes on people's feet without changing posture. Another clerk had to get the shoes off the shelf.

"I've only read one Hemingway story," said Cousin Toivo, "but I liked it a lot. Did you ever read 'Big Two-Hearted River'?"

"Sure," I said. "That's one of my favorites."

"It takes place north of here in the Upper Peninsula," said Toivo.

"In Seney," I said.

"That's right," replied Toivo. "I've wanted to go there ever since I read about it. I'd like to fish where Hemingway fished. I'd like to go for trout in the Big Two-Hearted River."

My twenty-five-year-old cousin Toivo loved to fish, especially for brook trout and rainbows. He was the outdoor type, but I was surprised he'd ever read anything by Hemingway. He'd only gotten to the ninth grade before they'd expelled him for punching a teacher. At fifteen he was already working full-time in the woods with his stepfather. At sixteen he had his own horse named Diablo and drove his own car—a fifteen-year-old black Oldsmobile with four-inch red dice dangling from the rearview mirror. I couldn't remember ever seeing him read anything—not even the newspaper. Somewhere, though, he'd read "Big Two-Hearted River."

"'Big Two-Hearted' is my favorite story," said Toivo. "I've read it twice."

"No kidding," I said, rather intrigued. "Where did you read it?"

"We had to read it in eighth-grade English," said Toivo. "Don't you remember?" I had forgotten. "That old bitch Mrs. McDuffie gave us a big fat book full of really boring stories, but I liked that one. It was the only one I read. It made me want to be fishing with Nick. That was the name of the guy in the story."

"I know," I said. "There are other stories about Nick. A whole lot of them."

"Oh yeah?" said Toivo. "Maybe someday I'll read another one. What I'd like to do tomorrow, though, is go to Seney and fish the Big Two-Hearted River."

"How far is it?" I asked.

"It's farther north than I've ever been," said Toivo. "I checked a road map. It's at least two hundred miles. We'll have to get up really early and make it a two-day trip. We can take a tent and camp out just like Nick did."

"Sounds great," I said. I didn't tell Toivo that the Big Two-Hearted River wasn't in Seney. Hemingway conveniently moved it for his story. I didn't care if we never found it. I just liked the idea of a day off.

By the ungodly hour of four A.M. the next morning we were driving north along I-75 toward the Mackinac Bridge that links Michigan's two peninsulas. When I told Cousin Toivo about the bridge—that at five miles in length it was the world's longest suspension bridge—he immediately became agitated. At the bridge approach he pulled over and parked underneath a huge NO STOP ON BRIDGE sign and ordered me to drive.

"What's the matter?" I asked.

"I can't trust myself on the bridge," said Toivo. "I don't know if I can hold the lane. What if I drive right over the edge? We'd drown for sure."

"That's impossible," I explained. "I've been over it before. There's a curb on both sides and an island in the middle."

"You drive," insisted my cousin.

Cousin Toivo is one of those guys who are completely in command in their own environment and completely displaced in someone else's. A couple of years ago my uncle drove Toivo into Detroit to take a three-week training course for future insurance salesmen. Toivo spent all three weeks in the hotel—ate in the cafeteria, shopped for souvenirs in the little shop off the lounge, and drank Stroh's in the bar. He saw nothing wrong with that—said proudly that the hotel contained everything he needed. "Besides," he said to my uncle when my uncle picked him up for the long drive back to Gaylord, "Detroit is full of crooks and black people." Cousin Toivo knows nothing about black people. I'm not even sure he's ever seen one. He just knows they're different and Toivo doesn't trust anyone that's different. If he had his way, everyone on earth would be a Finn.

Just for the hell of it I stopped the car squarely in the middle of the bridge. "Isn't that a great view?" I pointed out as we swayed back and forth.

"Oh yeah," said Toivo as he clutched at the dash so hard that his knuckles were turning blue.

"Just think. We're halfway between Hemingway's Walloon Lake and Hemingway's Seney."

"Yeah," said Toivo. "It's great. Now get me off this god-damned bridge or your ass is grass."

After we crossed the bridge Cousin Toivo insisted on driving again. "You never know what you'll find on these Upper Penin-sula roads," he explained. "Some of these unknown drivers are apt to be strange." We drove along the top of Lake Michigan past miles of empty beaches and past the edge of the Hiawatha National Forest to the north. We stopped for a breakfast of coffee and smoked chubs in the little fishing village of Naubinway.

An hour beyond the bridge we came to M-77, a secondary road that would lead us to Seney twenty-five miles to the north. "There weren't any roads like this when Hemingway came here to fish," I said.

"Oh yeah?" Toivo replied.

"His family used to take a ferry boat across Lake Michigan from Chicago in order to get to their summer cottage near Petoskey," I explained. "Up here there weren't any paved roads then. Supplies and people reached the nearest point by boat and then were carried or hiked overland."

"The fishing must have been great," replied Toivo.

Soon we passed a whole town for sale—homes, a store, a cocktail lounge, tennis courts. Down a small grade we passed

Lake Anne Louise and began to climb. We passed a MOOSE CROSSING sign which caught the eyes of both of us. Michigan had only recently imported moose into the Upper Peninsula from Canada.

"Keep your eyes open," said Toivo. "Seney's not far now, and we may cross the Big Two-Hearted River around the bend. Hemingway didn't say which direction the river was from the town."

Soon we passed a Mennonite church surrounded by old junk cars, then the Mead Creek State Forest Campground. A trailer sat beside the creek. Farther on we passed a canoe rental and then a huge sign on a tiny bar that exclaimed GOOD FOOD. Soon we entered a small settlement made up of two Mormon churches, the Eagles Nest Family Dining, and a ramshackle store whose sign proclaimed BOOK BARGAINS, JUNK, AND APPLIANCE REPAIR. Toivo was getting nervous. "Christ!" he growled. "Where's the river? Where's the wilderness? Where's the great fishing?"

"Time changes everything," I said. "Hemingway's Nick was here way back in 1919 or thereabouts."

"Rivers don't move," growled Toivo. "The Big Two-Hearted still has to be somewhere around here."

We were only about five miles from the town of Seney when we passed a huge sign for the Seney National Wildlife Refuge Visitor Center. This was soon followed by the Wigwam Picnic Area, Holland Creek, and then Seney itself. In the boom days of the lumber industry in the nineteenth century, Seney was full of hundreds of lumberjacks. Bars and whores were everywhere. I knew what we'd find now—a virtual ghost town. Seney was so small it hardly qualified as a community. There was a gas station, a small store, and a motel. The street was deserted—no pedestrians and not even a parked car.

Toivo pulled in at the store and the two of us went in to ask directions. The clerk, the only person on the premises, looked at us as if we were crazy. "I've lived here all my life and I never heard of a Big Two-Hearted River," he said. The clerk was a very old man. "You sure you don't want the Fox? Most folks around here fish the Fox."

"I can fish an ordinary river like the Fox any time," said Toivo. "The Big Two-Hearted is special. Ernest Hemingway fished there."

"He wrote a story about it," I added.

"Never heard of it!" insisted the old clerk. "Who's this Hemingway anyway? He from around here?"

"He was from Chicago," I explained. "He came here to fish right after World War One."

The old man stared at me distrustfully and then turned in upon himself. I could see a distance in his eyes as he searched back through the years. "I think it was 1919," he said at last. "There were three of 'em. Young guys from Chicago. One was just a kid. They fished the Fox for a week and caught a lot of brookies and rainbows—maybe two hundred in all. Two of 'em were about my age—maybe a little older. I'd've been twenty. The town was different but already small. Folks back then still remembered the lumbering days."

"How could you remember that?" I asked. "It was so long ago."

"Sure it was," said the clerk, "but I spent some time with them. We didn't get many visitors in Seney back then. They came in on the train. I'd been working in the woods that summer, but I was my own boss, so I took a day off to show 'em the best stretches of the river for trout. One of 'em—I don't remember which—asked a lot of questions about the old days, about the times the town burned, about the lumbering, and so on. If I remember right, the one with all the questions was a newspaper man. I remember telling him about one of our local characters—a guy who took a pocketful of frogs to the bar every night and would bite the head off one of 'em for a free drink."

"That couldn't've been Hemingway," said Cousin Toivo with conviction. "He didn't write newspaper stuff. He wrote stories— like in books. The one I read was about the Big Two-Hearted."

"That's right," I added. "We both read it. He tells about fishing the Big Two-Hearted right here in Seney."

"Maybe he did but it must have been in a different Seney," said the old man vehemently. "There's no such river around here. Anyway, none of those fellows that I remember was named Hemingway."

"Do you remember any of their names?" I asked.

"Nope," said the old clerk. "The names escape me. I think one of 'em may have begun with a *w*—Wemedge or something like that. An odd name." I sort of gasped at that revelation. Wemedge was one of Hemingway's nicknames when he was a young man yet unknown to the literary world.

"Let's get out of here," said Toivo. "I just drove a couple of hundred miles to fish the Big Two-Hearted and I'm going to find it."

"I'd try the Fox," said the old clerk.

Toivo stormed angrily out of the store and back into the car. He sat behind the wheel fuming, wondering what to do. Seney's single street remained empty. I sat on the passenger side and waited. I didn't want to interfere. After all, it was Toivo who had suggested this trip. It was he who had chosen to drive two hundred miles in order to fish for Hemingway's trout. I wasn't much of a fisherman myself. I'd rather read Hemingway's books than go fishing with him. I liked the clean polish of Heming-way's sentences—the way they seemed to re-create the actual emotions that accompanied an action. That re-creation was enough for me. I didn't need reality. Reality always included mosquitoes, wet feet, sweat, and dirt. I'd take the fictional fishing world of Hemingway every time over the reality. In reality Hemingway seemed to be an arrogant bastard who drank too much. If Hemingway were with Toivo and me right now, he'd've turned our fishing trip into a competition—into a race to see who could catch the most fish and the biggest fish in the shortest time. I'd read enough about him to know that. So I just sat and said nothing. I was happy we'd met the old clerk, though. He'd make a nice cameo portrait and a lovely literary anecdote for the other graduate students back at the university in the fall.

Finally Toivo had made up his mind. "Maybe the river is west of here. Let's try that."

"The old guy said the river doesn't exist," I said as Toivo swung the car westbound onto Route 28.

"What in hell does he know?"

"He's lived here all his life," I answered. We sped westward on a paved road that must have been laid down by a surveyor's rule. We drove 26.5 miles in an exact straight line on a road that never once went up or down. Beside the road flowed a perfectly straight muddy canal with banks so level that the grass almost seemed to have been mowed. "Maybe that canal's your river," I joked.

"Shit," said Toivo. We approached a container truck. Tailgating the container and hidden by it was the local sheriff. We were doing ten miles an hour over the speed limit. In seconds the sheriff had swung around, put on his flasher, and pulled us over. He gave us a forty-dollar ticket—payable immediately. As Toivo dug into his wallet the sheriff noticed our fishing gear on the backseat.

"Any luck?" he asked. Toivo and I just shrugged.

"Been fishing the Fox?" asked the sheriff.

"The Big Two-Hearted," I said.

"Never heard of it," said the sheriff. "That around here?"

"I guess not," I said.

We drove back toward Seney. "Your friend Hemingway is a liar," said Toivo bitterly. "I really believed in him but he's no different from all the rest."

"All the rest?" I asked.

"Everybody," said Toivo. "Like the guys who work in the mill yard. I have to keep double-checking their measurements so they don't cheat me."

"Hemingway was a storyteller," I said. "They're all liars. That's what storytelling is."

"Hunh," said Toivo.

"Maybe Hemingway just invented the river," I said. "Or maybe he moved it from somewhere else. Maybe it's north of here. Or east. Writers do stuff like that."

"He was a liar," growled Toivo. "We'll have to fish somewhere else. And not the Fox! Let's try that lake that we passed south of here—the one that's by the town that's for sale."

"Lake Anne Louise," I said.

We'd been fishing beside M-77 for about two hours. M-77 sat on fill that cut Lake Anne Louise in half, and so we were standing on the bank of the road and casting into the weeds along the two shores. We were hoping for bass but all we'd caught were two tiny yellow perch and a bluegill. Toivo was so disgusted by the prospects that he was beginning to mutter about giving up fishing for the rest of his life. "Maybe we should go back to that nameless bar with the GOOD FOOD sign and get ptomaine poisoning," I said.

"Why don't we just get drunk?" he replied.

A little Japanese car came over the crest of the hill behind us just as a moose suddenly blundered out of the forest and into the middle of the lane. The driver had no time to brake or to change direction. The little car slammed broadside at sixty-five or seventy miles an hour into fifteen hundred pounds of meat, bone, and guts. The impact ripped the moose open from front to back and flipped the massive carcass onto the hood. A minute later, when Toivo and I inspected the wreck, we saw at a glance what had happened inside the car. In a split second the full weight of the beast smashed into the windshield, scattering beads of glass onto the floorboard, the front seat, and the laps of the two occupants. All the gore from the split moose burst from the carcass to drench the occupants in moose muck—lungs, stomach, bowels, pancreas, everything.

For several seconds the car skidded dangerously, tire rubber screeching, as the driver froze the brake to the floor. The car shuddered to a halt no more than fifty feet from where Toivo's car sat by the side of the road behind us.

The driver and his wife were probably in their sixties. The car plates said they were from Ohio. Tourists. Their vacation was over—their car was a wreck, they were a wreck. Clothes, shoes, face, hair—moose muck saturated everything.

The old lady stumbled out and stood in the road in a daze. Remembering my Boy Scout training, I led her to the lake shore and laid her down on a level grassy spot. I elevated her feet and wrapped her up in an old blanket Toivo kept in the backseat.

The old man kept circling his wrecked car, saying nothing. Toivo picked up our fishing gear and tossed it into the backseat of our car. Then he opened the trunk, unsheathed his gutting knife, and advanced upon the old man, who began to whimper as he backed down the road, terror growing on his face. I left the woman and ran toward Toivo, grabbing his shoulder and twisting him toward me. "What are you doing?" I shouted. "You're scaring this old guy to death!"

Toivo stopped and looked down with dawning comprehension at the long knife in his hand. "I just need his permission," he said. "He hit it. It's his goddamn moose. But in this state they give every DOR to a state institution."

"What are you talking about?" I asked.

"Dead on the Road. The Department of Natural Resources gives every hit deer, bear, or moose to a local hospital or jail or old folks' home. That's fifteen hundred pounds of meat we're in danger of losing. I just need to ask this old guy if he wants the hindquarters, if I can have them."

The old man was still backing down the road as if he were deaf and blind to everything except Toivo's long knife.

A car approached from the south, slowed, and stopped. The driver rolled down his window. "You need help?" he asked.

"You could call somebody at the nearest phone," I replied. "We'll maybe need an ambulance too."

"I'll do that," said the driver, and he continued north.

"Damn! He'll call from that place just up the road," cried Toivo. "Come on and help me!"

Toivo rushed to the dead moose and began to slice at the hindquarters. His razor-sharp knife quickly severed one haunch and then the other. He and I together carried the meat to our trunk and heaved it in. The two haunches filled it.

"Let's get out of here," said Toivo.

"Are you sure?" I said.

"Help will be here shortly. These old folks will be okay," said Toivo. "Besides, what more could we do to help? I'm a damned good woodsman but not a doctor."

We drove east toward the Mackinac Bridge and home.

"Well, we got some moose meat anyway," I said.

"Yeah," Toivo said. "If Hemingway hadn't invented that goddamned Big Two-Hearted River, I guess we wouldn't have gotten it. You know, maybe he was right to move that river to Seney. That place is so damned dead that it needs some new geography just to liven it up."

"It's a good thing you read that story," I said.

"Yeah," said Toivo. "The moose meat'll sure help with the food bills. My three boys will be able to eat it for a couple of months. They can take moose sandwiches to school and impress their friends."

"Maybe you ought to read another Hemingway story," I said.

"Good idea," said Toivo.

"Maybe somehow we'd end up with another moose haunch," I said.

"If I could get a freezer full of meat for every story, I'd read every damned word Hemingway ever wrote," said Toivo.

"Hemingway has some stories about Spain and about Paris, France," I said. "Maybe you should read those and we could go to Europe next."

"Seney's far enough," said Toivo. "Too far."

"Maybe we'd get a bear haunch on the Champs-Elysées in Paris, France," I said. "Or maybe we could get some bullshit at the bullfights in Spain."

"Go to hell," said Toivo and began to laugh. "I'll leave the bullshit for you smart-assed college kids who can ask for it in Spanish."

"I'll drive the bridge," I said.

"You're goddamned right you will," said Toivo. "And you won't stop in the middle! And tomorrow morning you'll be up at five to take that load to the mill yard!"

Hemingway and Women

The boyhood girlfriends in Michigan:

Katy Smith of St. Louis. Her family had a nearby cottage. She was twenty-five, Ernest seventeen. Later she married John Dos Passos.

Prudence Boulton. A local Indian. Ernest may or may not have slept with her. Probably not.

Marjorie Bump. A Petoskey girl who was a lot of fun.

The first love:

Agnes Von Kurowsky. She was an American nurse in the hospital in Italy where Ernest was recovering from the wounds he received in World War I. She was twenty-five, he eighteen. Later she became Catherine Barkley of *A Farewell to Arms*.

The wives:

Hadley Richardson from St. Louis. Attended Bryn Mawr. She married Ernest on September 3, 1921, in Petoskey. She was twenty-nine, he twenty-one. Her suicide father and her grandfather left her a permanent income from endowments. The money was sufficient to allow the Hemingways to live in Paris and to take vacations in Switzerland and Spain. They had a son, Bumby.

Pauline Pfeiffer from Piggott, Arkansas. Graduate of the University of Missouri. She met Ernest in Paris while she was a fashion editor for *Vogue*. When they married, she was thirty, he twenty-six. They had two sons, Patrick (1928) and Gregory (1931). Pauline's family was wealthy. Her uncle bought the Hemingways a beautiful home in Key West.

Martha Gellhorn from St. Louis. Attended Bryn Mawr. A foreign correspondent and novelist from a distinguished family, she met Ernest in Key West and later joined him as a reporter covering the Spanish Civil War. She married Ernest on November 21, 1940. She was thirty-two, he forty-one.

Mary Welsh of Bemidji, Minnesota. She met Ernest in London while they both were correspondents during World War II. Both were married at the time. After the divorces, they married on March 14, 1946. She was thirty-eight, he forty-seven.

Other women:

In 1922 Ernest was unfaithful to Hadley while covering the Greco-Turkish War from Constantinople.

Lady Duff Twysden. A twice-married alcoholic party-goer and flirt, she accompanied Hemingway and friends to Spain and later became Brett Ashley of *The Sun Also Rises*.

Jane Mason. Married, rich, and beautiful, she and Ernest had an on-again, off-again affair while he was married to Pauline. She was supposedly Pauline's close friend.

Marlene Dietrich. She and Ernest were close friends. He affectionately called her the Kraut.

Adriana Ivancich. Ernest met her in Italy in 1946. From an upper-class titled family, she was beautiful and seventeen. He was forty-seven. She became Renata of *Across the River and Into the Trees*.

On safari in East Africa with Mary, Ernest and a Masai woman named Debba broke the camp bed.

THERE IS NO SMYRNA, ONLY IZMIR!

Margaret kicked out desperately and pumped her arms as hard as she could, but the cold dark undertow pulled her inexorably downward and outward. Above, the shimmering, crystalline surface withdrew and she knew without doubt that she was going to die.

She woke bathed in sweat and several seconds passed before the grogginess receded and she realized that her mother was calling her for school. For another minute she lay still, aware now that the sheet had twisted itself about her bare legs. Then she sat up, unwrapped her legs, and swung them to the floor. The dream was still vivid, still frightening.

Margaret hated to begin another day. It was too early. Her tired body protested. Her back muscles ached and she could feel another headache coming on. The thought of once again speaking and listening to Turkish caused a faint throbbing and a tightness somewhere above and slightly behind her temples.

At least it was Friday. One more day and she'd be through another week at Atatürk School for Girls. Last night had been bad. She had slept fitfully, in part because the ugly cinderblock walls of her family's apartment magnified sounds. She hated the apartment for that reason. She'd just started to fall asleep when she heard those hateful sounds through the wall—the third time in a week. She knew what it was—the young Turkish couple next door trying to make another baby to add to the four they already had. Margaret had rolled to the side of the bed away from the wall, but it hadn't done any good. She could hear everything— almost as if they were in *her* bed. Then she had thought of Ahmet Bey, the physics teacher, and she had almost died of shame. She couldn't help herself. She thought of him constantly— his azure eyes, his sleek walk (like a large cat), his thick mane of dark chest hair. She adored his mustache. Every Turkish man she'd ever seen had a mustache, but Ahmet Bey's was special—a light tan line in beautiful contrast to his dark wavy locks.

Margaret rose and went into the bathroom. As she prepared for the day she could hear her parents out in the kitchen. Her mother's voice was shriller than usual, her father's calm. They were talking about the possibility of war with Greece and about the arrest on Wednesday of Mustafa Bey, her father's friend. Mustafa Bey was the chairman of the philosophy department at Ege University. He and Margaret's father, Frank Maki, had become close friends shortly after the Makis arrived from America six months ago. Frank Maki had replaced the director of the American library in Izmir, Frank's first overseas posting as a State Department employee after twelve years in Washington. Shortly after Frank's posting, he had been contacted by Mustafa Bey, who was working on a new philosophy textbook for Turkish lycées and who needed to use the American library for research. On the recommendation of the government, Mustafa Bey had added a chapter on Marxism. Then the military overthrew the elected government, sent machine gun–toting soldiers into Mustafa Bey's classroom, and arrested him as a leftist agitator. No one had seen him since, but everyone knew how the military treated

accused Marxists—they were beaten, tortured, sometimes exe-
cuted. Immediately after the arrest, Frank Maki made inquiries
to the military governor. Margaret hoped he had heard something positive. Mustafa Bey's daughter, Ayşe, was in Margaret's
class at Atatürk School for Girls. Margaret liked Ayşe, but since
Mustafa's arrest the two girls had been awkward with each other.
Margaret felt deep concern for her friend, but Ayşe perpetually
looked on the verge of tears, and Margaret dreaded a scene.
Then there was the presence of Melek, another classmate and the
daughter of the regional governor. Melek's father had surely
issued the order for Mustafa Bey's detention.

It was all so confusing. In fact, everything in Turkey confused
Margaret lately. The day before, the girls had planned the
humiliation and resignation of Ahmet Bey, and now Margaret
would never again see his adorable mustache and the curly hair of
his chest. Why had the girls done that? In her halting Turkish,
Margaret had asked her friend Müge, but Margaret had not
understood Müge's reasoning. Müge said it was an insult to the
girls—that the principal should never have hired a male teacher
for a girls' school. Margaret had thought Ahmet Bey an excellent
teacher and still felt anger as she recalled the events of yesterday.
Melek, the flirtatious one, had used the five-minute break between classes to go to the toilet after history class. Then, just as
Ahmet Bey was beginning his physics lesson, she had reappeared
and Margaret had gasped. Melek had replaced the usual gray
skirt of the official uniform with a much shorter and much
tighter one of an identical gray. Melek then sat in the front row
right in front of the teacher's desk, crossed her legs vivaciously
and, while staring hard at Ahmet Bey, began rhythmically to
rock her leg back and forth. For a while Ahmet Bey ignored her,
but his eyes finally caught hers. Melek immediately shouted,
"Why are you always trying to undress me with your eyes!"

Ahmet Bey had turned scarlet. Then all the girls had begun to shout. Gradually the sound grew into a roar and Ahmet Bey had rushed out of the classroom toward the principal's office. An instant later Melek had dashed to the toilet, to reappear moments later in her regular skirt. Ahmet Bey had not returned. He had resigned and had left the campus.

The girls had found this episode wonderfully entertaining, and, as the story spread throughout the school, Melek had become a hero. But not to Margaret. To her Melek was someone frightening, someone who hurt others—just like her father the general. Margaret noticed that Ayşe had not participated in Ahmet Bey's humiliation. In fact, Ayşe had stared at the floor as the other girls shouted, and her eyes had glistened with tears.

Now Margaret had to go back to that school, had to try again to communicate in a foreign language with girls whose actions she didn't understand. Margaret wondered what new craziness would disrupt today. A new American teacher, a Peace Corps Volunteer named Lars Olson, had arrived the month before to teach English at Atatürk School for Girls. Now that Ahmet Bey had been driven out, Lars was the only male instructor of a faculty of thirty-eight. The Turkish girls didn't seem to think there was anything wrong with Lars's being there but Margaret now wondered if he too was in danger.

In the kitchen Margaret sat down to a Turkish/American breakfast of cornflakes from the NATO commissary and black olives and rose jam on toast. "Have you heard anything about Mustafa Bey?" she asked her father.

"I talked to the military governor," her father replied over a cup of very black tea. "The governor wants the American government to ask for his release. The military can save face that way. They know they made a mistake."

"But that's weird. First he orders the man's arrest, and then he wants you to get him out of prison." Here we go again, Margaret thought. The day is just beginning and everything is getting strange. Margaret's father looked up from his tea and smiled but said nothing. Margaret wondered what the smile meant. Was he laughing at her spontaneity or at the severity of her school uniform? Her long blonde hair nearly dipped into her dish as she rushed to finish her breakfast.

"I told your father he should have demanded Mustafa Bey's immediate release." Margaret's mother had been angry ever since the arrest. Later in the day she planned to visit Mustafa Bey's wife. They were going shopping together and then to the beach at Kuşadasi. Turkey had wonderful beaches—hundreds of miles of white sand. And ruins. Everywhere along the coast were the remnants of the past of the Greeks, the Byzantines, the Ottomans. Margaret and her mother both loved the ruins. The food too was magnificent. Margaret's favorite was börek, goat cheese mixed with eggs and rolled up in a thin dough. Her mother's was fish kebab. Margaret and her mother often spent Saturdays together enjoying the delights of Turkey while Mr. Maki worked.

"We'd better hit the road. I have a lot to do today." Margaret's father warned his wife to be very careful during her visit with Mustafa Bey's wife. "If there are soldiers around, stay out of their way," he urged her.

As Margaret and her father came out of the apartment building, they saw two rough-looking soldiers lolling on the corner, occasionally waving down a car and searching it. "The girls say the soldiers take bribes from everyone they stop," said Margaret as she and her father got into the Ford with embassy plates. "They won't stop us, will they?"

"I don't think so," replied Frank Maki. "They'll see the plates and leave us alone. If they do, speak only English and don't smile."

The trip to school was uneventful except for a long wait at Rumeli Caddesi while a seemingly endless military convoy passed. It was very hot. Margaret tried the radio, but all the music was non-Western. "Where are they going?" Margaret asked but didn't expect her father to tell her. She suspected he probably knew—or at least he had a good idea—but he kept that sort of information to himself.

This time he surprised her. "They're going to the Greek border," he said. "There's a lot of trouble on Cyprus, and Turkey may invade soon. If they do, it could cause a war with Greece."

"Do you think that will happen?" Margaret recalled the endless political discussions at school. All of them ended with the girls listing everything Turkey would do to Greece if the Greeks caused any trouble over Cyprus. Melek in particular was adamant about Turkish rights to the northern half of the island and about Greek crimes. She always acted as if she had inside information—as if it were the habit of her father to confer with her concerning future actions of the army. Yesterday she had said that Turkey would take Cyprus on Saturday. That was tomorrow. Such an invasion would ruin Margaret's plans to go to the beach. Her parents would make her stay inside. Saturday night there would be a curfew and a blackout. Sunday would be the same. The whole weekend would be ruined. Melek had also hinted to Margaret that the American government favored the Greeks and ought to be punished. "If Henry Kissinger were here," Melek had said, "I'd make him into a eunuch." The other girls had laughed loudly. Margaret had pretended to join them, but her face had been fiery hot and inside she was angry. She hated the fanatical patriotism of Melek and of the school authorities. She remembered the bulletin boards, always covered with portraits of Atatürk surrounded by miniature Turkish flags. She remembered the sayings of Atatürk that bordered the blackboard. She remembered the morning assemblies where all the girls sang the national anthem. Most of all she remembered the five minutes of total silence that commemorated the moment that Atatürk had died in 1938. She and the others stood at silent attention in the assembly area by the school flag. Some girls wept afterward. Margaret now knew that when she returned to the States she could never again salute the flag and listen to "The Star-Spangled Banner" without thinking how stupid all such ceremonies were. Previously she had never given American patriotism a thought, but Turkey had changed that.

They arrived at the school with only minutes to spare before the morning assembly and roll call. Margaret piled out of the car, grabbed her book bag from the front seat, and slammed the door. She waved as her father drove away. Then she turned toward the gate and stopped short. In huge letters with white paint someone had written KILL KISSINGER across the red gate. Margaret wondered whether the message were meant for her or, more probably, for the Peace Corps teacher. Why was it written in English? All sorts of crazy thoughts began to whir through Margaret's mind. She suddenly remembered the story about the American who had bought a car in Turkey from another foreigner, but in order to register the car the American had had to drive the vehicle to Greece and sell it to himself for a dollar. Why? Margaret couldn't imagine. And she remembered the other girls' stories about life at the university where rival student political gangs sometimes shot it out in the cafeteria or the classroom while other students lay on the floor, under desks, under tables. She thought of the two suicides in this year's graduating class—both girls preferring death to the marriages arranged by their parents.

Ali Bey stood by the gate as usual, checking every girl as she passed and ensuring that no young men got into the walled-in campus. Ali Bey was a villager like all the maintenance crew. He was short, plump, and gnarled. On his gray locks sat one of those pancake hats popular throughout Turkey's villages as a replacement for the fez banned by Atatürk after World War I. Ali Bey always wore a flannel shirt winter and summer and thick wool jodhpurs held up by suspenders. As Margaret entered, Ali Bey bowed deferentially, showing her the same fawning respect he reserved for the teachers. He bows to money, Margaret thought. He thinks I'm the daughter of a rich American. She hated this obvious sign of the tight class structure that formed modern Turkey.

Now Ali Bey was motioning to her, indicating her hair. She had forgotten to pin it back. The school code was very strict about hair. If she were Turkish, she would be severely punished, but as an American she could feign ignorance at least once and get away with it.

The campus was lovely, a kind of Eden walled off from the crowded, bustling port of Izmir. It was an odd Eden, however, for there were no Adams, only rich Eves, the daughters of the wealthiest people in the city. As soon as Margaret walked through the gate, she entered a privileged world. Even the air smelled better, perfumed by the herbal hedges that lined the walks and by the fruit trees beyond the tennis courts. Margaret hurried past the outdoor theater, left her books against the wall inside the door of her classroom, and went off to the morning assembly.

She knew the ritual well and abhorred it—the roll call, the checking of uniforms for unbuttoned blouses and improper skirt length, the checking of hair length, the raising of the flag, the singing of the national anthem, the recitation of some words of Atatürk, the presentation of the day's schedule, and finally the marching in columns to the classrooms.

As Margaret joined her classmates, she wondered what would erupt today. She could sense tension in the other girls. It must be the approaching war, she thought. If Turkey invades Cyprus, they'll hate me. What will they do to me?

In Lars Olson's English class, the Turkish girls sat erect, backs stiff and necks taut. Their eyes sighted along flared nostrils. Margaret crouched in her seat, the heat of the room burning into her back. Or maybe the heat came from their angry eyes. Lars Olson didn't seem to notice, but how could he not? The anger struck the back of Margaret's head like a thousand tiny needles. Her neck ached.

When Lars had arrived from Minnesota a month earlier, the school principal quickly explained what Lars was not to do. "Never mention Armenians, Greeks, Marxism, Christianity, or these writers." The principal handed Lars a long list of names of forbidden writers. Lars glanced at it and noticed Saroyan. He read it then and was surprised to see Steinbeck and Hemingway. He could understand how Steinbeck might make such a list since he had once been controversial in America. But Hemingway? He decided that very day to teach Hemingway's censored journalism about the Greco-Turkish war, and now the opportunity had come.

Lars Olson finished reading aloud the first two Hemingway essays, "Old Constan" and "Refugees from Thrace." Now he was about to read "On the Quai at Smyrna." He cleared his throat, lifted his eyes from the text, and smiled. The girls glared defiantly, their long hair tied back in the regulation manner. Every schoolgirl in Turkey wore her hair just like that. Every schoolgirl also wore a uniform, this one being a dull gray skirt with a high-collared white blouse. Periodically the Turkish vice-principal lined up the older girls and measured their skirts with a meterstick. If the skirt did not reach to the curve of the knee, the girl was sent home. When she returned she spent hours on a hard bench outside the vice-principal's office before she was given permission to rejoin her class. Still, some of the girls had shortened their skirts just enough to indicate a bit of thigh. The girls in the front row were even braver. In the confines of Lars's classroom they felt safe from the prying eyes of the vice-principal and of her spies. They had unbuttoned the top buttons of their blouses so that a tiny bit of soft white flesh was visible. Melek was the bravest. She had unhooked three buttons to show a piece of bra strap and cleavage. She was satisfied that, in spite of her showy anger, Lars Olson's eyes had twice roved in her direction. Lars, however, had heard the stories about Melek's role in the demise of Ahmet Bey, and he was careful.

None of these daring flirtations registered on the stony faces of the other girls. They were as impassive as coal. Some had been like that since Lars's arrival.

"The next piece should interest you a lot," said Lars into the silence. "Hemingway was on an Allied ship during the evacuation of the Greeks from this city in 1922. This short piece describes the evacuation through the eyes of a British officer who was there when the Turkish army torched the Greek and Armenian quarters."

Margaret could feel the hatred building up—surrounding and isolating her as an American. As Lars began to read again, she rose fearfully and glided to the front of the room. Her ears and face were burning with embarrassment below her blonde hair. She stood for what seemed an eternity just to the left of the teacher's desk. Finally Lars paused and recognized her. "They're really angry," she whispered.

"I know, Margaret," he replied quietly. "It's good for them. Now return to your seat."

Margaret did not hear the rest of the reading. Her chest hurt. Oh God, she thought, why did I have to leave the United States? Why did my father come here? She was terribly afraid now—afraid of what the Turks would do to her when the class ended. Why did Mr. Olson do this? Didn't he know that the girls liked him, that some professed to love him? They talked all the time about his blue eyes and wavy blond hair. He was the only man on the faculty and now they would hate him as they had hated Ahmet Bey. They would drive him away. And her too. It was all the fault of Hemingway. Why did he have to write terrible things so that the government would censor his stories?

Thank God, Lars Olson had stopped reading. Now he was speaking to the class in his clipped Minnesota nasality. "I want a discussion," he was saying. "Are there any comments?"

Margaret's friend Müge was on her feet, her legs tight together as if she were about to spring. "Mr. Hemingway is a liar and a fool," she said in a high-pitched voice. "He says the streets of Istanbul are muddy, but they are paved!"

"In 1922 they were not paved," replied Lars.

Müge sat down abruptly but other voices began to shout from all over the room. "He calls Istanbul by the Greek name of Constantinople! That's wrong! Our city is not Smyrna! It's Izmir! He's a friend of the Greeks! A terrible man! As bad as your President Wilson who tried to give our country to the Armenians!"

Müge was again on her feet. The other girls ceased abruptly. "Sir, Mr. Hemingway is a terrible writer. He never tells the truth about our country. He hates Turks. Our government is correct in not allowing us to read these awful stories."

"Thank you, that's enough," said Lars. "You may sit down, Müge." But Müge stepped up onto her chair and stretched her arms out in front of herself as if she were conducting an orchestra.

"There is no Smyrna, only Izmir!" she shouted, waving her arms in the air as the other girls joined in. The cries reverberated off the walls as Margaret hunched ever lower in her seat. She attempted a wan smile, but it fell from her face when a girl in the next row hissed in her direction. Margaret wanted to hide, to disappear forever from this school and this city. "There is no Smyrna, only Izmir!" the voices cried in unison while Lars Olson stood in stunned disbelief behind his desk.

The bell rang. The shouting instantly stopped as the girls rushed pell-mell past Margaret toward the open door. Lars Olson followed the last out the door. Margaret could see him through the window as he trudged up the hill toward his bachelor apartment. He looked big and awkward with his load of books. Like a bear, she thought, but they used to like him. Now I must screw up my courage and go outside to face them.

The Turks were full of their usual gaiety as they waited for their next class by the fountain in the courtyard. They were jabbering excitedly about their boyfriends, the latest fashions, last night's movie on television, the weekend's activities. These were modern girls. Outside the school they wore blue jeans and T-shirts and drank Coca-Cola.

Margaret approached a group and waited to see what would happen. Her hands were shaking and her chest still hurt. She tried to listen but the Turkish jumbled in her head. She wished they would speak more slowly. Sometimes she understood almost nothing, which made it easy for them to tease her. They didn't seem to understand that she had only been in Turkey a short time and that the language was very difficult.

Melek broke from the group to join Margaret. "We all saw when you walked to his desk," said Melek.

"I only wanted to warn him that you were angry," replied Margaret.

"You're such a fool!" exclaimed Melek, but her voice was not harsh. Then Melek laughed. "We had to teach him a lesson, that's all," she said. "He was so sure of himself. Anyway, all of us read those Hemingway pieces years ago. Does he think we're children? We're seventeen."

"You've read them?" asked Margaret in disbelief.

"Of course. We always read anyone the government bans—Steinbeck, Miller, Lawrence, Arden. I've read them all."

"But I thought they were not . . ." Margaret searched for the Turkish word and then gave up and said "obtainable" in English.

"We cannot buy them in Turkish," replied Melek. "We read them in English. We can read it quite well, you know, even though we rarely speak it. Listen, do you think we made him angry?"

"I don't know," replied Margaret evasively.

"I think he's cute, don't you?" asked Melek.

"He's old," said Margaret.

"Oh, no," exclaimed Melek, shocked. "He's not over thirty. My fiancé is thirty-six. He owns a chemicals factory in Ankara. He's much older than Lars Olson and not half as romantic. Still, he has his way and my family likes him a lot. My father calls him his son—his rich son."

Margaret didn't know what to say. Besides, she now had a booming headache. The Turkish issuing from Melek's mouth was like the screech of a chain saw chewing through Margaret's brain. It wasn't that Margaret disliked the language. In fact she found it quite beautiful. But now her brain seemed to have overloaded on it, and she desperately needed to go somewhere quiet and dark where the onslaught of words could dissipate.

Other girls joined Melek and Margaret. Melek and the others began avidly to discuss Lars's male qualities. They giggled frequently.

Müge had been standing aloof from the group, but now she joined them. She smiled at Margaret as if to say, "We're still friends." In English she told Margaret that they ought to go to the beach together on Saturday afternoon if the invasion did not occur. Then she spoke to the gathering in Turkish. "Cocuklar . . . çocuklar . . . we must be careful now. Treat Lars Bey very nicely for the next few days. Don't forget that he's the only single foreign male they've ever allowed to teach here. If we drive him away, we'll never get another. He is not a common villager like Ahmet Bey. We must treat him like a gift from Allah."

The bell rang. The girls rushed noisily into the next class, Margaret with them. Thank goodness, she thought, this is math, a universal language. She would not need to strain so much to understand the Turkish. Maybe her headache would go away. Maybe she would survive in Turkey in spite of Ernest Hemingway.

HEMINGWAY AND SPORTS

Ernest was not a great athlete. He inherited a weak left eye from his mother that inhibited his depth perception and that cut down on his ability to shoot or to do similar activities. In high school he finished next to last in cross-country runs, managed the track team, and made the second string of a mediocre varsity football team only in his senior year. He learned to box with friends in his mother's music room but was slow and clumsy. An excellent fisherman, he treated the sport almost like a religion. Because he loved all sports, he wrote about boxing; fly fishing; deep-sea fishing; hunting for deer, grouse, bear, elk, and African big game; baseball; bullfighting; bicycle racing; swimming; boules; football; horse racing; tennis; skiing, lugeing; hiking; canoeing; and camping.

Hemingway is considered by many to be one of the great sportsmen of our time and certainly the greatest one among writers. Stories abound about his athletic prowess, many started by Ernest himself. Some of these stories border on the ridiculous but have been accepted as true by his friends, reporters, critics, and biographers.

For example, Hemingway told Archibald MacLeish that he learned to box on the tough streets around his home, that he

44

injured his eye in a fight in Waukegan. He told someone else that he learned to box in a Chicago gym, that he had a number of semipro fights, that he worked as a sparring partner, that he became an honorary member of the Mafia at nineteen. He said he once broke his hand during the weekly fights at a Billings, Montana, whorehouse. Another time he became upset during a championship fight because the champ had fouled his opponent. Ernest jumped into the ring and knocked out the champ.

Ernest also said with great solemnity that he could hit a tennis serve that didn't bounce.

A SHORT UNHAPPY LIFE

Although I'm now past forty, people are still surprised by my boyishness—by the eternal adolescent who peers out at them through thick glasses. The glasses correct weak eyes, especially my left, which kept me out of Vietnam and out of the service altogether. None of this would be important, I suppose, if I had never read Hemingway's very negative comments about eternally adolescent American males. Hemingway grew up at the turn of the century—a time when Teddy Roosevelt was the role model for every red-blooded American boy. Both Teddy and Hemingway hated military shirkers. Hemingway himself had a weak left eye which kept him out of the American Expeditionary Force in World War I, so he joined the Red Cross and served in Italy. In his third week he sustained 227 wounds from mortar shrapnel and two wounds from machine gun bullets. I admire him for being all that I am not. I'm indecisive, cowardly, unathletic, uncreative, and almost obsessively clumsy. Hemingway was the opposite—brave, sporting, literary, and lusty enough to have had four wives. He spent his creative years examining men facing death. I'm terrified of death and go out of my way to avoid thinking about it. I like my world to be quiet and safe.

I was first introduced to Hemingway and to his fictive world in a story called "The Short Happy Life of Francis Macomber." Francis was terrified of lions, but I'm afraid of everything. I'm a panaphobe of the worst kind. That's why I went to school for so long. I knew I couldn't survive in the real world. Eventually I got a doctorate in literature but even then I avoided reality. I still teach in the same Midwestern university from which I graduated. It's not a particularly well-known school. In fact it's third-rate, which is fine with me because it takes the pressure off. I teach a couple of classes and periodically write a grant that supports post-doctoral studies that I never complete.

I lead a bachelor life of quiet desperation and steady mediocrity. I cook gourmet meals for myself and my girlfriend and cheer frantically for the Cubs. They never win and that satisfies me. If they were to win, I don't think I could handle it. I have a lot of difficulty supporting winners.

My girlfriend of sorts is Tiffany, a crashing bore with a degree in developmental education. She works only with the stupidest students but calls them developmental learners. Every fall Tiffany tests every student that previous tests have shown to be reading below the eleventh-grade level. She then places these students in various reading programs. As the semester progresses, she plays statistical games, raises all students' reading levels by three or four grades in three months, congratulates them and herself, and then begins the process all over again with the next batch.

Tiffany and I have had a lot of loud disagreements about remediation. My own view is that people who can't read should not be in college. But why do I vent my anger against Tiffany? It's all wasted since she never replies. She's not much different from her students. For her all civilization prior to the Beatles does not exist. She doesn't know dates either. She believes all dates are irrelevant unless they come to your door bearing a bouquet. That's a hint that I never bring her flowers. She's right. I never do.

Whenever I get too depressed by such thoughts, I escape once again into the world of Hemingway's fiction. I've read the complete works at least fifty times, and I always begin each re-reading with "The Short Happy Life of Francis Macomber." I first read that story when I was an undergraduate taking freshman composition, in 1963. We were assigned the story on November twentieth. I read it on the evening of the twenty-first, and the following day, when we were to discuss it in class, events in Dallas erupted and I never did get the professor's interpretation of what happened on that long-ago African morning before the war. The professor still teaches here. He's now a doddering old man who barely remembers his own name. His students complain constantly about boredom. Although I pass his office every day on my way to my own, I have never stopped to ask him for his interpretation of "The Short Happy Life." Whatever it is, it wouldn't help now.

Since that November in 1963 I have been haunted again and again by the same Technicolor, Cinemascope image. A child of the movies, I always envision the final scene of Hemingway's story in Hollywood terms. On the far left of the screen Margot Macomber is perched above the plain, sitting forward on the rear seat of the open motor car. Looking a lot like Joan Bennett of United Artists' *The Macomber Affair*, she is still holding the smoking Mannlicher against her right shoulder. Her elbows are supported by the back of the front seat. In the center of the screen Francis Macomber's body is crashing rightward into the dry veldt grass. The top half of his skull—blood, brain, bone—is exploding outward, drenching in dark drops the wiry grass and the dusty earth. To the far right the buffalo is plunging leftward onto his front haunches, the entire weight of his massive body tipped into the earth. The buffalo's body plows a furrow in the plain, raises a red cloud. Oddly, Wilson is not in the scene. Wilson is the British guide—the man of action who takes charge of everything throughout the safari. It is he who tells us that Margot intended to kill her husband, that she is a murderer. But then he has good reason to say so. He dislikes Margot and Margot has something on him that could lose him his license: she knows that he stalked the buffalo illegally with the vehicle.

For well over twenty years I've been haunted by that scene and by the similar scene of Lee Harvey Oswald, leaning his elbows on that window ledge in the Dallas Book Depository and sighting on a cheerful President Kennedy below on the rear seat of an open motor car.

Lee Harvey Oswald, that son of a bitch, is probably the ultimate cause of my dilemma. If it weren't for him I might have discovered in 1963 whether or not Margot meant to shoot her husband. In 1963 I was only nineteen—still young and naive enough to accept whatever a professor wished to palm off as the truth. Unfortunately, I never got the truth. Instead I got a terrific headache and spent the day wandering about the campus in a migraine daze, trying to avoid TV sets and radios with their repetitive message of sudden death. The first full-fledged hero of my short life was dead, and all I could think about was Francis Macomber. In my grief I even got the deaths mixed up. I pictured John F. Kennedy lying face down in waist-high grass somewhere in Africa, the back of his skull imploded by the force of an African safari rifle. Simultaneously I pictured Francis Macomber, a boyish grin frozen on his youthful face, pushing his whole body into the plush leather of the backseat of an open limousine. Bullets were splattering Francis's face into oblivion as

Jackie and Margot sat beside him, smiling prettily for the cameras and wiping bits of gore from their faces.

There's nothing I can do about the past now—about the way I am trapped forever with two entwined deaths on November twenty-second of 1963. The perplexity is there and will remain there, deep in my soul, in spite of my current efforts to discover a definite answer to at least one of the deaths, Francis's.

Since 1963 I've probably read "The Short Happy Life of Francis Macomber" five hundred times and have taught it every year since 1969. I have an almost desperate need to know what happened as if, by knowing that, I will know myself. That's why months ago I decided to put an ad in a paper. Not just any paper either. I put it in the personals section of the *New York Review of Books*. I figured that *Review* readers would be sophisticated enough to figure out what I wanted. I was wrong, of course. Readers of the *New York Review* are no brighter than anyone else. They just have bigger egos—the kinds that are spawned on the East Coast.

This was my ad: "Desperate Francis seeks beautiful bitch named Margaret for buffalo hunt." You'd be amazed at the crazies who replied. I received dozens of letters, most from the New York area but at least one from as far away as Yankton, South Dakota. Most correspondents were sexually aroused by misconceptions of what I meant by a buffalo hunt.

I gave up on the ad and decided to call everyone named Margaret in the Dubuque, Iowa, phone book. I chose Dubuque because it's a macho place in the Hemingway tradition. A hundred years ago buffalo roamed by the millions around there, and the city still has a famous meat-packing plant. Unfortunately, the first twenty-three Margarets thought I was an obscene caller and hung up. I became worried about their reaction and my phone bill.

In desperation I advertised in the newspaper of the university where I teach. This time I worded the ad carefully in order to avoid perverts: "SWM seeks beautiful bitch named Margaret for literary experiment. GOOD PAY." The initial reply was from an alumnus who raised hounds. He said he didn't have a bitch named Margaret but he was willing to sell one named Elvis.

The second reply was from a graduate student in computer science named Kimberley, who said she'd do anything for good pay if it wasn't too kinky. In her reply (which contained four misspellings and one *gonna*) she said that most people found her "physically desirable." She informed me that she had waist-length blonde hair, blue eyes, large breasts, a "happy" personality and "liked to read, especially Stephen King." In her spare time she swam and hiked. The work *hiked* caught my eye. Obviously the young lady lacked Margot Macomber's sophistication, but that really wasn't important. Mainly I needed someone who was physically active, and this one would do. I phoned her.

The next day Kimberley chewed a pack of gum very rapidly throughout the interview. She wore a metallic-blue jumpsuit with a tiny silhouette of Michael Jackson on the breast pocket. She answered all questions in a tiny high-pitched voice similar to those tinny voice boxes in dolls. I couldn't bear the thought of having her take the role of a Hemingway heroine.

Finally, I gave up all pretense of objectivity and visited Tiffany. I told her that I wanted to reenact the last scene from the Hemingway short story that I had read to her several years ago. Tiffany herself rarely read anything beyond her *Reading Techniques* text. Still, she knew for certain that she ought to loathe Hemingway. She had heard somewhere that he was a male chauvinist pig and insisted that he was not only overrated but that his writing ought not to be taught. She and I had argued about this on everal other occasions. "But you're judging the man without having read what he wrote," I said.

"That's not true," she replied. "I read that thing with that horrible woman in it and that's enough. Hemingway hates women."

"You can't judge a writer from one short story," I said. "Besides, you didn't read that story. I read it to you. I wanted to read you his other African story too—'The Snows of Kilimanjaro'—but you wouldn't let me. I know why. You must be the only person who ever found 'The Short Happy Life of Francis Macomber' to be boring. If you had let me read you the second story you would have discovered that the woman character is very strong in an admirable way and that the dying husband is weak and self-pitying."

Tiffany ignored my argument and reiterated her position. "Any feminist knows that Hemingway fails to create believable women," she replied. "*Ms.* says so. So why should any woman bother with his writing?" Tiffany often uses a reference to *Ms.* the way that fundamentalists use the Bible—to shut up the opposition. She doesn't read *Ms.* but she uses it as a convenient weapon in arguments.

Tiffany turned on a Jane Fonda tape, cranked up the volume, and began her aerobics. I dropped into a chair, thrust my palms over my ears, and waited.

After what seemed an eternity Tiffany turned off the tape and stopped gyrating. She picked a towel from a pile of dirty laundry half hidden behind a chair and began to wipe beads of sweat from her brow. "Why don't you get that story out of your head and go on to other things?" I followed her into her apartment's tiny kitchen where she dug through the freezer in search of an errant TV dinner. "I know it's in here somewhere," she said as she pushed aside boxes of broccoli, French fries, and cod fillets. Finally she emerged with a little paper box. She tore open the end, pulled out the little plastic dish, and popped it into the microwave on the corner of the sideboard. "Do you want anything?" she asked.

"A gimlet," I said.

"I have Coke," she said.

While Tiffany ate pasta covered with some sort of bubbling gray paste, I sat opposite her at the kitchen table and drummed nervously on the can of Coke with the fingers of my right hand. "I've got to know whether or not Margot murdered her husband," I explained again. "Damn it, Tiffany. Can't you see that this is important to me!"

"I don't want to play Margot," said Tiffany.

"There's no one else who will do," I said.

"What does that mean?" asked Tiffany. Her eyes narrowed into hostile slits. "Margot was a terrible woman!"

"She was a bitch," I said. "Good God, Tiffany, I'm not asking you to *be* her. I just want you to act the role. You be Margot and I'll be Francis." I took a big gulp of Coke as Tiffany swallowed the last of the gray-coated pasta and dropped the empty dish into the open garbage can. After placing the dirty fork in the sink, she took a cup from the dish rack, filled it with tap water, and popped it into the microwave to heat it for her coffee.

"Who will be the buffalo?" Tiffany asked as she sat down with her coffee. "And what about that white hunter guy—the one who slept with her?"

"To hell with Wilson," I snapped.

"Okay, so maybe we don't need a hunter for me to sleep with, but a buffalo is indispensable." Tiffany laughed and rolled her eyes. "They're kind of cute."

"I haven't solved the buffalo problem yet," I said.

"Write a grant," she suggested.

*   *   *

The National Endowment for the Humanities gives fellowships
for literary research, but competition for the limited funds is
terrific. I'd had success in the past in applying for such grants,
but this time no one in Washington was impressed. One of the
three unidentified referees wrote that he hoped *I'd* play Francis,
a not too subtle hint that I ought to be shot in the head for
dreaming up such a scheme. The second simply wrote, "You
gotta be kidding! Do we really have people like this teaching in
our universities?" The third, who must have been a real jerk,
wrote that my project was "imaginative and admirable" but that I
needed "to identify my objectives and costs more clearly."

I decided to plan the reenactment without outside funding. I
went to a local gun shop to inquire about renting or buying a
Mannlicher 6.5, the weapon that Margot had used to kill Francis.
The clerk, who was also the shop owner, looked surprised by my
request. "What do you want it for?" he asked. He was a little guy
with a Marine Corps haircut and the kind of bright startled eyes
found on a steer after a sledgehammer has caved in its forehead.
He wore a red flannel hunter's shirt, Army fatigues, and running shoes.

"It's for a literary project," I said and knew immediately that I
had given the wrong reply. The clerk peered at me suspiciously
as if I were some new kind of kook. "I want to kill a pest," I
hurriedly added.

"What kind of pest?" asked the clerk.

"A buffalo," I said.

"Exactly what kind of buffalo?" asked the clerk.

"African," I said.

"Cape?"

"Yes."

Obviously the clerk didn't trust me. Not only had I indicated that a Cape buffalo was digging up my garden or knocking down my fence or some such thing but I had also shown my complete ignorance of firearms. Hemingway would have dismissed me in a second. He might even have punched me out. At the very least he would have told me to get the hell out of the shop. Fortunately the clerk kept his aplomb. He probably dealt with people like me every day since there are a lot more of us in the world than there are of Hemingways.

"A Mannlicher 6.5 will certainly not do the job," said the clerk in the kind of tone usually reserved for small children.

"Why not?" I asked.

The clerk dug around below the counter and soon produced a catalogue with a picture of a Mannlicher on the cover. "A Mannlicher 6.5 is a light weapon with a very light cartridge. It would be fine for shooting a deer or something smaller, but not for shooting a Cape buffalo unless the hunter were absolutely accurate. I hunt every fall and practice frequently, but I'd never go after a buffalo with a Mannlicher. I'd get gored. That buffalo would run right over me, and I wouldn't even slow it down with those cartridges."

"Would a Mannlicher kill a man?" I asked.

"Sure," he said, "but I wouldn't advise it." The clerk looked me up and down and then peered directly into my eyes with such intensity that I was forced to look away. "You aren't one of these Lee Harvey Oswald types, are you?" he asked.

"Do I look like one?" I said.

"You look like a rabbit," he replied.

"Tell me more about the gun," I said.

"A Mannlicher is short and light. A woman could handle one

without difficulty. So could some skinny guy like you. The rifle was popular in Africa in the old days but it hasn't been made since the early sixties."

"Can you get me one?" I asked.

"Oh, sure," the clerk replied, "but it'll cost you a pretty penny. I may have to look through *Shotgun News,* a trade journal. They're occasionally advertised in there as collectors' items. Does it have to be in good condition?"

"I want it in such good condition that Ernest Hemingway would approve," I said.

The clerk's voice lost its gunmetal hardness and sounded friendly for the first time. "Then it had better be like new," he said. "It'll probably run you twelve hundred dollars. The cartridges are still manufactured by Norma, a Swedish outfit. They're expensive—about twenty-five dollars for one box."

"Good God!" I exclaimed. "Isn't there some cheaper way? Could I rent one?" I suddenly felt trapped among the rows of deer rifles that lined the shop walls. All those rifles but not one Mannlicher.

"Are you kidding?" replied the clerk. He reached into the display case and pulled out a box, opened it, removed three long brass shells, and laid these in a row on the open palm of his left hand. With the fingertips of his right hand he began to caress the shells. "Feel these," he said lovingly. I reached out and touched the hard cold metal. "These are very similar to the shells of a Mannlicher." The clerk put the shells away, picked up a catalogue from behind the case, shuffled through the pages for a few minutes, found what he was looking for, turned the catalogue toward me, reached around, and thrust his index finger again and again at one of the pictures. "That's a Mannlicher," he said. "Take a good look at it. People spend thousands of dollars to possess such a rifle. They invest a good part of their lives in order to own such beauty and workmanship, and you say you want to rent such a weapon. You insult all owners of Mannlichers. You insult me. You insult people like Ernest Hemingway. He owned a Mannlicher. Would Hemingway have rented his rifle or his fishing pole? Hell no! He loved his possessions. Renting a Mannlicher and owning a Mannlicher—it's the difference between a twenty-minute trick with a street-corner whore and your first teenage love. One is ugly; the other is holy."

"I'm sorry I brought it up," I said. I felt humiliated, the way an errant child feels before a wrathful parent. This energetic little man came only to my shoulder, but he terrified me. He was one of those people who do things. I was one of those who read about things but didn't have a clue how to do them. I felt like an incompetent idiot in front of him. Sweat poured into my eyes. I wanted to run away, but my feet refused to move. The clerk suddenly began to thrust his index finger against my chest. His eyes grew brighter and rounder, taking on the metallic sheen of newly minted quarters. "You're the kind of pasty-faced son of a bitch who's never been outside in his life, who'd trip over every root on the forest floor and snap every twig." I must have turned my body toward the door or indicated in some other way that I was about to bolt because the glow went out of the man's eyes as quickly as it had come. He became businesslike once again. "These guns are relatively rare. It may take me weeks to locate one. If we're lucky, it'll only be a couple of days."

"I guess you'd better order me one," I said. "Have you read Hemingway?"

"Of course," The clerk looked as if I were a fool for asking. "I owe Hemingway everything—my interest in guns, my hunting as a hobby, my shop. When I was a kid I happened to read *Green Hills of Africa*. That's what got me started. After that I read the rest of his stuff and then branched out to reading famous

African hunters of the turn of the century, people like Baron von Blixen and Captain Stigand. As soon as I was old enough I took up hunting. That first year—I think I was fourteen—all I had was a single-shot twenty-two, but I managed to bag a couple of partridge and some rabbits. After that there was no stopping me. It was guns, guns, guns. And I owe it all to Hemingway—to that initial reading of *Green Hills*."

"Then you've read 'The Short Happy Life of Francis Macomber,' " I said.

"Oh, sure. Years ago," said the clerk. "That's the one where the wife murders her husband." I hated the clerk then. How could he, a man with a limited knowledge of literary criticism, state with such certainty what had happened? Not only had he previously made me feel like an incompetent fool who didn't know how to do anything but now he was trying to tell me that I didn't know how to read anything either.

"How do you know?" I asked. "Maybe she meant to shoot the buffalo but accidentally hit her husband."

"Are you joking?" The clerk laughed in that way that parents have of laughing at a small child who has just said something stupid. "Of course she murdered him. She blew the brains right out of that yuppie son of a bitch!" The clerk sounded as if the same should happen to me.

"Prove it," I challenged. I was now angry and felt like punching the little guy. Instead, I took off my glasses and wiped them on my shirt front. They had become partially fogged from the sweat that ran down my forehead and salted my eyes.

"It's simple." The clerk once again punctuated each word by thrusting his index finger into my chest. "She wanted his money. If she couldn't control him, she didn't want him around. Besides, she hit him right in the base of the skull. Nobody shoots that well if they're not aiming to kill. Try it. You'll see what I mean. Plus Wilson says she did it."

"But Wilson is unreliable." I felt like I was about to lecture a student once again, to point out to some errant undergraduate the flaws in his reasoning. I wanted to take charge, to be the teacher, but I was too terrified of this little guy. He reminded me vaguely of all the serial killers I had ever heard of. He was aggressive. He used threatening language and abusive gestures. He owned and loved hundreds of guns. He considered me a wimp and hated me for no reason at all. He probably sought the meaning of life through his membership in the NRA.

"Are you disagreeing with me?" asked the clerk. "I hate people who disagree with me when I know I'm right. How can people be so stupid?" The clerk took an air pistol out of an open case, aimed it at an invisible target on the wall behind me, pretended to fire, and pretended a recoil.

"Wilson distrusts Margot with her desire to control all those around her—to control Wilson too, by threatening to tell the authorities about his use of the motor car during the hunt."

"You mean the way he pursued the game with the vehicle?"

"Yes," I said.

"That's not just bullshit," said the clerk. He picked up a cleaning rod, aimed it at a point between my eyes, sighted along it, said, "Pow," and then set it back down on the counter top. Then he began to lecture at me, treating me as if I were the dumb one. "A white hunter's reputation was everything back then. He paid only a pound a license and yet few people qualified to receive one. The government checked each would-be hunter's character very carefully, you see, and most chaps weren't up to par. Any disparaging rumor—proven or unproven—could cause the license to be lost. The government was colonial and a sort of law unto itself. It didn't need absolute proof of poor conduct. Yes, Wilson really was in danger of losing his livelihood if Margot had pushed the issue upon their return to Nairobi."

"And yet you still assume that what Wilson implies is true—
that she murdered her husband," I replied.

The clerk was indignant. Once again he picked up the cleaning rod from the counter top. This time he banged it on my left
shoulder, as if he were knighting me, each time he made a point.
"I don't base that solely on Wilson's words," he growled. "I base
it on the whole story—on Margot's need to dominate, on her fear
of abandonment during the final hunt, on her refusal to deny
Wilson's accusation after the shooting. She was a bitch." I turned
to look out the window, to see if anyone was passing who might
help if this crazy little man suddenly attacked me. There was no
one on the street. I stepped back toward the door, where the
cleaning rod couldn't reach me. The clerk noticed and smiled, as
if he were delighted to see my fear. All this time he continued to
lecture at me. "Margot shot him. Nothing simpler than that.
Plus she shot him with a Mannlicher, a sort of popgun to a
buffalo but a very effective man killer. If Hemingway had
wanted her to be shooting at the buffalo, he'd have given her
something heavier, such as a .375 Holland and Holland Mag-
num. They've been making those since 1912, and they were very
popular in Africa in Hemingway's time. A .375 would knock a
buffalo to its knees even if the shot wasn't clean." The clerk put
the cleaning rod away and began to fiddle with his fingers on the
counter top.

"What about a Springfield?" I asked. "Would that stop a
buffalo?"

"Probably not. It would certainly be more effective than a
Mannlicher, but I wouldn't use one."

"Well, what would you think of a white hunter who would
give his client a Springfield on a buffalo hunt?" I asked.

"I'd say the white hunter was either incompetent or had some
other reason for giving the guy a relatively light weapon. After

all, the client is supposed to be doing the killing. The white hunter is just there as guide and backup. Therefore the client should have a heavy weapon."

"How much would a Springfield cost?" I asked.

"Oh, there are still plenty of those around. I have one right here in the shop that's in good condition. It'll cost you an additional four hundred dollars. Do you need one of those too?"

"I don't know yet," I said.

"You don't know a helluva lot, do you?" asked the clerk. "When are you going on this buffalo hunt?"

"I don't know," I said. "I wasn't planning on spending so much money. Also I still have to find a buffalo."

"I can't help you there," said the clerk. "You'd better look in a zoo. Cape buffalo don't roam in your average suburb, you know. They're all in zoos in this country."

The Indianapolis zoo had an African buffalo, but the director wouldn't let me borrow it. In fact, after I asked, he wouldn't even let me near it. He explained that the buffalo was an extremely valuable animal, quite rare in the United States, and that it was presently not on exhibition because it was the mating season. "But you have only one buffalo," I said.

"That's correct," replied the zoo director. "You see, our one animal is a female and when she's in heat she gets very agitated. We're confining her so that she doesn't inadvertently damage herself."

"When can I see her?" I asked.

"Maybe in a couple of weeks," said the zoo director.

As I was leaving, one of the keepers approached and walked with me to my car. "I overheard the conversation," he said conspiratorially. "How much is it worth for you to see the buffalo?"

"Fifty bucks," I said.

"You're a weird son of a bitch," said the zoo keeper.

I chose not to reply. The keeper was a burly man with a face the color and texture of raw beef. He probably outweighed me by fifty pounds.

"Why do you need to see the buffalo?" the keeper asked.

"I need to time it," I said.

"What do you mean?" asked the baffled keeper. "This isn't some weird kind of sex thing, is it?"

"I need to know an African buffalo's acceleration rate and its top speed," I said. "It's for a literary experiment."

"The hell it is," sneered the keeper. "Why don't you just look it up in an African buffalo book?"

"I don't think there is such a book," I said.

"Hell, there's books about everything," replied the keeper in disgust.

"Not about that," I said. "I know. I teach in a college."

"Aha! That explains your weirdness," exclaimed the keeper. "It'll cost you a hundred bucks and we'll have to do it after closing hours. At seven tonight I'll be on duty—sort of a night watchman. I can let you and the buffalo into the exercise yard. What'll you measure the speed with?"

"I'll borrow a speed gun from the college baseball coach," I said. "I've already checked with him. It's okay."

"We'll have to figure out a way to get her running," said the zoo keeper.

"We could scare hell out of her with one of those big air horns off a truck," I said.

"You got one of those?" asked the surprised keeper.

"Hell no," I said, "but I'll get one by tonight."

"Weird," muttered the zoo keeper. "Really weird."

*   *   *

That afternoon I borrowed the speed gun and bought an air horn at a used auto parts yard. Then at 6:30 I picked up Tiffany, who insisted that she wanted to see the buffalo. We were at the zoo by seven and the keeper let us in immediately. He was dressed in an outfit from the Banana Republic catalogue—khaki T-shirt with the company logo on the front, khaki shorts with a half dozen pockets. The outfit was meant to remind one vaguely of Hollywood's idea of East African dress in 1920. Obviously Tiffany was taken in by the uniform. Or maybe it was the keeper's beefy build. The guy had a massive hairy chest and bulging muscles on his arms and legs. When he walked he bobbed from side to side and leaned slightly forward on the balls of his feet, as if he were about to lunge at somebody's throat with his teeth. Whatever the reason, Tiffany was smitten, and I regretted having brought her. "Is that the official zoo uniform?" I asked.

"This? I ordered it from a catalogue," replied the keeper. "It's a little company that has a lot of stuff suitable for a guy like me." The keeper's voice rasped like the wings of an attacking insect, and as he led us across the yard to the buffalo he pirouetted several times on the toes of his heavy leather jungle boots as if he were showing off the latest fashion for the well-dressed ape.

The exercise yard lay somewhere to the rear of the zoo. The keeper had already transferred the buffalo from her cage to a holding pen in the yard.

On our walk through the zoo Tiffany and the keeper got along famously. Several times they laughed uproariously together; as they walked ahead, I could hear them whispering as if they didn't want me to hear.

Around 7:30 we let the buffalo into the exercise yard. She was old and mangy, her mating days obviously long over, but she still managed to accelerate at an amazing rate when I blasted the air horn right in her ear. The keeper, from the far end of the yard, worked the speed gun as she came fast as a crab right at him, her massive head straight out and her eyes bloodshot. Tiffany stood off to the right with a pen and pencil and hurriedly scribbled numbers as the keeper shouted them. When the keeper realized that the buffalo was going to run right over him, he dropped the speed gun and made a mad dash for the protection of the shed door. In full charge, however, the ancient buffalo died. The spirit was gone, the immense carcass pitched forward, slid on its haunches for another five yards, and lay still, about two yards behind the fleeing back of the terrified keeper.

Seeing what had happened, I began to jog toward the far end of the yard, a distance of perhaps fifty yards. Panting heavily by the time I arrived, I first inspected the buffalo carcass, noting the creature's ugliness in death. Then I picked up the speed gun and checked figures with the keeper. He had recovered his courage and was now strutting around the dead beast as if he were the victorious hunter and not, as had been the case a moment earlier, the hunted. "Tiffany and I have to go," I said as I grabbed Tiffany's arm and propelled her in the direction of the gate, behind which sat our waiting car.

"Hey! Wait a minute!" yelled the keeper, suddenly aware of his plight. "We've got to get this carcass back in its cage or I'll lose my job!"

"No time now!" I shouted over my shoulder as we hurried away.

Halfway across the yard, Tiffany broke away from my grasp and turned back toward the keeper, but I caught her arm firmly and yanked her in the direction I wanted to go. Behind us the keeper was dancing in a trance around and around the dead buffalo as if he were trying to exorcise a demon. His massive hairy arms whirred ineffectually about the beast like disconnected windmill blades in a gale. "The silly bastard looks like a gorilla in a Jungle Jim suit," I said as I pulled Tiffany inexorably toward the yard exit and the runway beyond. The keeper shouted one last plea in our direction. "Please help me. I'm only one guy. What in hell am I supposed to do with something as big and heavy as this dead buffalo?"

"Hemingway would eat it!" I yelled back.

In Hemingway's final scene the wounded buffalo charges out of the bush toward Francis Macomber. Francis gets off three quick shots with the Springfield before Margot blows Francis's brains out with the Mannlicher from her position in the open motor car. The mortally wounded buffalo drops dead a couple of yards from Francis's body. The eternal question—did Margot intend to shoot the buffalo or her husband? Hemingway tells us that she meant to shoot the buffalo. Can I believe him any more than I can believe Wilson? Does he have any more control over his characters than God seems to have over us? After all, Hemingway wrote the story at a typewriter in the study of his home at Key West, far from the African veldt. Can I trust Lee Harvey Oswald? Didn't he use a Mannlicher too? Was that in the Warren Report? Is that report real or fictional? Can I trust it? Can I trust anything or anybody? Do the authors of these crimes— Hemingway and Oswald—and their victims—Francis and Kennedy—only exist to confuse me? Are the worlds they inhabit equally real and false? Are their worlds any different from this one? Where is the difference? I am frightened. All of these worlds seem to exist only to confront me, to destroy me.

And what about Jackie's pink hat? Is it any different from the bits of pink flesh and pulverized brain at the back of Francis's head? Why did she choose that color for Dallas?

I returned to the gun shop and bought the Springfield.

*   *   *

The clerk tried to talk me into buying additional guns but I resisted. Afterward he was quite helpful. He showed me how to load the rifle and how to fire it. I bought several boxes of ammunition and practiced quick-firing technique at a firing range. I asked Tiffany to come along. She used a stopwatch to time each burst of three shots. Once I got the hang of it, we took the average of ten bursts and figured that must be close to Macomber's time as he fired at the charging buffalo.

The buffalo in the Indianapolis zoo had hit sixty-five miles per hour just before she died, and that was from a standing start of slightly less than fifty yards. I sat in my office with a calculator and tried to figure out the relationship of the buffalo's speed to the time that Macomber spent in firing. The relationship would show me how far the buffalo was from Macomber when it began its charge. I also hoped to figure out how much time remained from the moment that the buffalo appeared to the moment it would have gored Macomber.

The unknown factor was the distance of Macomber from Margot. That had to remain an approximation. Nothing more. Hemingway says Macomber, Wilson, and the middle-aged gun-bearer walk until the gun-bearer is sweating profusely. Of course they walk slowly and carefully because the thick brush is hiding a dangerous animal, but how far is that walk under a tropical sun? How long does it take for a middle-aged African native to sweat profusely? I can't know.

I took my results to Tiffany. "I've got the timing pretty much worked out," I told her. "I'll have to approximate the distance of your target from the car. Now all we need to do is have you stand in the back of an open Jeep in the middle of a hay field with the Mannlicher beside you. I'll signal with a whistle that the buffalo has begun its charge. I want you to try to pick up the Mannlicher, jack a shell into its chamber, aim, and fire before the buffalo can reach Francis. I'll indicate that moment by blowing the whistle a second time. If you can manage all of that between the blasts of the whistle, we'll assume she could have been aiming for the buffalo."

"So what?" asked Tiffany. "That doesn't prove anything."

"It proves she could have been aiming at the buffalo," I said. "But if you can't get off the shot in the allotted time, that means Margot must have already picked up the Mannlicher before the buffalo charged. That would indicate that she was already planning to shoot before anything happened."

"That would mean she murdered him," said Tiffany, completing my thought.

"Precisely," I said.

The next afternoon Tiffany and I drove a rented open Jeep into a farmer's field not far from our campus. I walked about fifty yards ahead of the parked Jeep and set up one of those cardboard silhouettes of a man that police departments use to train officers. My silhouette was cut from a stiff-backed, life-size poster of Michael Jackson that I'd pilfered from a music store entrance-way. I liked the idea of having Tiffany blow a hole through her hero. I wanted her to feel as empty afterward as I did when President Kennedy died. Tiffany stood silently in the back of my Jeep as I walked out there and propped Michael up in the knee-high grass. I had left the Mannlicher leaning against the edge of the seat beside her.

I trudged back, positioned myself about ten yards to the right of the Jeep, and brought a referee's whistle to my lips. "When I blow, go into your act!" I shouted.

"I'm ready!" replied Tiffany. She didn't seem to care whose silhouette she was about to shoot. In fact, she barely glanced toward Michael. Instead she nervously eyed the rifle. I could tell that she didn't like the idea of firing it, and her vulnerability somehow made her look even prettier as she stood there in blouse and jeans, the breeze ruffling her hair. I eyed my stopwatch and blew. Tiffany grabbed for the Mannlicher but it slipped from her hand and fell with a thud to the floor of the Jeep. "Wait a second!" she called. I watched as she repropped the rifle against the edge of the seat. "Ready!" she called again. I blew. This time she grasped the rifle firmly and hoisted it to her shoulder, but something happened—maybe her hand was shaking too much— and the shell jammed in the chamber. "I'm sorry," she said. "Can you fix this?" She held out the rifle and swung the barrel in my direction.

"Don't do that!" I cried, ducking aside. "Never aim a rifle at anybody!" I hurried to the Jeep and, with great difficulty and a lot of cursing, managed to unjam the chamber. This time I stood right beside the Jeep as Tiffany repropped the rifle once again against the rear seat.

"Ready?" I asked. Tiffany nodded. I blew. This time Tiffany grabbed the rifle, rammed its barrel straight into the floorboard, and, using the floorboard for leverage, easily maneuvered a shell into the chamber. She also accidentally pulled the trigger at the same time. The shot tore the weapon from her hands and ripped a neat round hole through the floorboard.

"What in hell are you doing?" I yelled as I climbed into the Jeep to stare in disbelief at the powder burns circling the frayed floor carpeting around the bullet hole.

"Look what it did," said Tiffany, holding up her bruised right arm.

"Look what you did to the Jeep!" I cried. "Jesus, can't you do anything right? What a screw-up! Lee Harvey Oswald never would have done that!"

Tiffany looked startled. "What do you mean?" she asked.

"Margot never would have done that!" I shouted.

"That's not what you said before," said Tiffany.

"Well, that's what I meant!" I said.

"Margot was a bitch!" shouted Tiffany. "She screwed up everything! All I did was put a hole in your goddamned rented Jeep! You don't even care about my arm!"

"I'm sorry," I said, suddenly realizing how unfair I was acting. After all, what did Tiffany know about guns? Nothing. She'd never fired one before today.

"We should have practiced," I said.

"There's no way I'm going to waste my time practicing firing a gun!" shouted Tiffany angrily.

"Okay, okay," I said. "Just one more try. Then we'll call off the whole thing."

"Promise?" Tiffany asked. I promised.

On her final attempt Tiffany chambered the shell first. Then she swung the rifle to her shoulder, brought the barrel to eye level, aimed, squeezed the trigger, and blew out the windshield. The ricocheting shot kicked up dust about eight inches from my feet. In all the excitement I failed to keep track of the time.

We drove back in silence. The Jeep dealer nearly had apoplexy when he saw the damage. He threatened to call the police unless I paid on the spot in cash. I paid. Tiffany and I got into my car and drove toward her apartment. "You know," I said, "this experiment has taught me really to admire Margot Macomber. I still couldn't tell you whether or not she murdered Francis, but she had to be an amazing woman just to get off the shot so cleanly."

"Only a bitch could do it so well," said Tiffany. "A nice girl like me isn't worth a damn when it comes to handling a big heavy gun like that." I laughed, but I knew inside that Tiffany really did consider herself that kind of nice girl—the kind that still has stuffed animals on her pillow when she's thirty-four. I wondered if she had a stuffed Cape buffalo.

"My experiment really flopped," I said. "It was nothing but a waste of time and money."

"What did you expect?" needled Tiffany. She took a file from her purse and began to smooth out a chipped nail. She seemed to be deeply engrossed but I knew it was just a front—she was really just trying to avoid further conversation. "I don't want to see you again," she finally said and stared out the side window.

"Christ!" I tried to sound hurt. I think I was, but mostly for reasons of pride. "You're going to leave me? Just like that?"

Tiffany didn't reply.

"Jackie never would have left Jack," I said. "Sure, she went off with that Greek tycoon, but that's only because her husband was dead."

"You're not making sense again," said Tiffany.

"Neither are you." I had a sudden urge to drive right off the road into the nearest tree, but I didn't because I knew the action would be misunderstood. Tiffany would assume I was suicidal because I couldn't bear the thought of losing her, and that wasn't the reason at all. I just felt empty—as if I were tumbling through an endless black hole. "Nothing's made sense since November 22, 1963," I said. "All my hopes and dreams were nullified by the bullet that blew out Kennedy's brains."

"I was only ten in 1963," replied Tiffany. "None of that meant anything to me. It still doesn't. You have an obsession. You know that?"

I began to pound my left arm hard into the door, clutch the wheel with my right, and shout over the wheel at the windshield. "Of course I know! Don't you think I know? I used to be happy!

Now I'm not! Something happened! Oswald! Margot! Hemingway! I'm all mixed up!"

Tiffany had slid to the far side of the seat and had one hand on the door latch as if she were prepared to spring out. "You're not a pleasant person." She almost whispered, as if she were afraid of my reaction. "You want to get inside Margot's and Oswald's heads, but you can't. Look inside your own head if you want answers. Even then you'll never know."

"Never," I said, gritting my teeth and settling back in the seat. I suddenly felt very tired. "Maybe we could have a quiet meal together and forget the whole thing."

"Not tonight," said Tiffany. "I have a date."

"With the zoo keeper?" I asked. "That goon?"

"He's cute in that safari outfit," said Tiffany. "Plus he didn't say nasty things to me. You've been really nasty lately."

We didn't speak again.

HEMINGWAY AND WAR

Hemingway sometimes told stories that made his entire life sound like a war. People believed him when he said he had ridden the rails as a boy, had dealt with tough guys and prostitutes, had tested himself against them, had lived in the Michigan woods like an Indian, had learned to speak Ojibwa.

In actuality he spent three weeks in July of 1918 on the Italian Front as a Red Cross ambulance driver. He was wounded while dispensing cigarettes and chocolate to Italian soldiers on the Piave. His wounds were serious—227 shrapnel wounds, two bullet wounds. He returned to his post in October but soon contracted jaundice. Sickness and injuries were numerous over the years. In Africa he suffered from amoebic dysentery and was in two plane crashes. He was in six automobile accidents. He frequently bumped into things with his head and accidentally shot himself in the leg.

He knew a lot about war since he served as a correspondent covering the Greco-Turkish War in 1923, the Spanish Civil War from 1936 to 1938, and both the Pacific and European theaters in World War II.

Myths about his exploits abound. Here are some of them, again often started by Ernest himself.

In World War I he said he led Italian storm troopers during an attack on Monte Grippa, that he was buried for three days by the explosion that wounded him, that after his wounding he threw away his pistol so that he wouldn't use it to end the pain, that he had twenty-eight bullets extracted without anaesthesia, that he was an infantryman in the regular Italian army, that he fought in major battles as a lieutenant of the *arditi*. He said the *arditi* were often ex-convicts who had committed murder or arson. A wounded captain plugged the bullet holes in his own body with cigarettes and went right on fighting.

He said he fought in the Turkish army against the Greeks.

He said that during the Spanish Civil War he lubricated overheated machine guns with urine, that he shot a truck driver who was taking priceless art from the Prado to Switzerland.

In World War II he bragged he commanded troops in engagements, had personally accounted for twenty enemy dead. He said he led eighteen Frenchmen against a German tank, suffering eight dead and two wounded. He said he landed on Omaha Beach, that he entered Paris first, that he busted the Siegfried Line, that he shot a POW who refused to be interrogated, that he was finally wounded by a direct hit of a tank shell.

IN A HOT SEASON

America.

I weep for you and for my lost innocence.

Millions of my generation grow up too fast on November 22, 1963, but I have already lost my political innocence in 1956 when, at the age of fourteen, I see Russian tanks in the streets of Budapest. America, you are a bumbling parent, a kind of groping giant that stumbles along helplessly until it's ten years too late. Then you lash out viciously in Vietnam, causing too much of the wrong kind of damage. America, you act like a Russian bully.

After the failure of the Hungarian revolt, I want to do something for the world, for my country, for myself. I want to rediscover the lost pleasure of giving without conditions. Suddenly worldly cynical, I long to be childlike again—to give the poor of the Third World a Christmas present in the form of myself. I want suffering humanity out there to know that there is still an American willing to help. I want to be proud of myself and of the nation that formed me.

I missed out on the liberation of Paris.

74

In 1957, at the age of fifteen, I read Henry Miller, D. H. Lawrence, Jean Rhys, and Jack Kerouac—the holy outlaws, the spiritual barbarians. I long to escape the little mining town in central Maine which I call home—to hit the road, to hitchhike all over the world. The farthest I ever travel is Boston. Once.

At Monson Academy I major in sports—basketball, alpine skiing, baseball. I make the All-State Team three times and somewhere between games and practices date a cheerleader who, even then, I know will grow up one day to become a kind of super secretary for some other guy. We have sex in common, nothing else.

After the tedium of high school classes, I welcome the social and intellectual freedom of college. I go to the state university at Orono to study literature. Every year there I discover a slew of writers new to me, among them Ernest Hemingway. Hemingway becomes my favorite author, my mentor, my idea of a macho man. I avidly read his works, completing the project with *Green Hills of Africa* in my senior year. I long to discover Hemingway's Africa for myself, the white hunter's Africa of grassy plains teeming with wildlife. I long for the adrenaline rush that comes from the thrill of the hunt. I long for the quieter pleasures that come from evenings of fellowship, strong drink and good food around a safari fire, followed by nights with a courageous woman like Mary in the same tent.

Later in my senior year I apply for the Peace Corps, fulfilling a vow I made to myself on the day President Kennedy died. On the three lines where I am to indicate my first, second, and third countries of preference, I write *Africa*. In the fall of 1965 I undergo two months of training for Nigeria at Michigan State University. A third month is spent in the black ghetto of Detroit where the very air tastes of violence, where people's eyes smolder. Two years later these streets will erupt into riots, looting, gunfire and sudden death. The ghetto will burn.

I go home to Maine for Christmas. On January 4, 1966, my sister drives me sixty miles through subzero temperatures and a raging snowstorm to the little airport in Bangor for a flight to New York. There I join twenty-eight other Volunteers for the long flight to Lagos via Dakar and Monrovia.

Somewhere over the Atlantic I fold up my winter jacket and squeeze it into the small suitcase I have carried aboard. A year and a half later I will remove the coat from the suitcase, will discover it has turned green with mildew and mold, will find small creatures embedded in the piling. I will plant the coat at the edge of the rain forest behind my house.

Among the twenty-eight Volunteers is Tanya. A year later I will marry her in the Catholic church that dominates the center of the bush village of Olona in the Midwest State of Nigeria.

Why will I do that? Even now I'm not sure. Maybe it's her spunkiness, her resistance to the norm.

Tanya is pretty but not beautiful. Her eyes are polished ebony and her hair shiny black. She looks sixteen when she is twenty-three. For a time this will irritate her, but years later she will still appear a young woman in her twenties when she is approaching forty. By then strangers will mistake me for her father.

A doctor's daughter from an elite northshore Chicago suburb, she will spend her life denying privilege. A product of Catholic schools, she will deny the authority of the Pope and actively oppose his positions on abortion, female clergy, and liberation theology. From a tightly knit family, she will war all of her adult life with her dominating and manipulative mother but will support that mother always when the mother is in turn dominated and manipulated by her doctor husband. A product of the staid Midwest, she will call herself a citizen of the world, will admire all cultures other than her own. Raised by a Republican father who considers Nixon a leftist, she will join the Democratic Party, will actively oppose the Vietnam War, and will march for civil rights. A socialist, she will see the Swedish and Yugoslav political systems as models for the rest of the world.

An active feminist who hates the manipulation of women by men, she will try to manipulate others as her mother manipulated her. She will try to manipulate her son and me. She will try to manipulate the whole world, to force it and all of its inhabitants into whatever mold she knows is best. The world and its inhabitants will not cooperate. Neither will her son. Eventually neither will I. This will make her angry. She will steam for years in that anger.

But that is in the future.

Right now I am attracted to her worldliness. She has studied in France, traveled in Spain, Italy, Yugoslavia, Greece, and Germany. She has wonderful stories about beer halls in Munich, Kennedy's speech in Berlin, spring in Delphi, and thirteen-year-old lechers in Italy.

She has plans—further study in France, an M.A. from Middlebury, a Ph.D from a prestigious university. Then she may marry.

I tell her I don't wait. There are plenty of women in the world. Right there on the plane is a six-foot-tall blonde Mormon who has been making a play for me since the day Peace Corps training began. I don't tell Tanya that Lynn, the Mormon, bores me with her endless monologues about the Church of Latter-Day Saints.

"Billy is willing to wait," Tanya says. Billy is supposed to be her current boyfriend. A wonderful pianist, he has played in the White House, including at Lynda Bird's wedding. Billy, however, is a momma's boy. Billy's mother has the imperial bearing of a concentration camp guard. Billy will never leave her or his music. A wife will be third in line. Tanya knows this. I know she knows and say nothing.

The rich fetid odor of decay permeates the humid air of Lagos. We spend one night there, at the airport hotel. The next morning we break into four groups and travel to our respective regions. Eight of us fly to Kano in the Northern State, where we will learn our specific destinations and schools. Mine will turn out to be teaching English and physical education at Bornu Teachers' College in Maiduguri. No one from the Peace Corps office has been there. Maiduguri is 540 miles away, connected to Kano by a one-lane ribbon of highway that runs endlessly in a straight line across the flat, semiarid plain. To the north is the Sahara Desert and the Republic of Niger. To the east lies the Republic of Chad and civil war. A day's drive from Maiduguri is Lake Chad, a Switzerland-size body of water right on the edge of the Sahara. The shoreline is a constantly shifting swamp teeming with wildlife—elephants, crocodiles, and millions of birds. In the evening the air vibrates, shimmers from dense clouds of mosquitoes. Local herdsmen dig grave-size holes in Lake Chad islands and cover these with layers and layers of tightly woven grass mats that keep out the mosquitoes. Here they sleep. Their cattle have huge hollow horns that act as water wings to support their heads as they graze and sleep in the lake, only their snouts showing.

In Peace Corps training we are told that Nigeria is the one former British colony in Africa where the British parliamentary system has succeeded. We are young and naive and believe the people who say this. We actually think they know something about Africa. Events prove they don't.

*   *   *

Kano is the largest city in the Hausa-dominated Northern State. The Muslim Hausa are small traders and farmers. They are proud and reticent—we greet them on the street and they say nothing. Fewer than one percent are literate. They scorn the Western values of the British who have dominated the region for a hundred years. In many ways their lives have not changed since Islam swept through this part of the world in the Middle Ages. They still farm with a short-handled hoe, travel by horse, keep their women in purdah.

That first night in walled Kano, two other Volunteers and I go exploring. Alan will teach biology in a place called Ilorin, Pam will teach math in Bauchi. They are fun-loving sorts who want to check out the local bars. Ten months from now Alan will be nearly beaten to death by a mob when he foolishly drives a car with Northern plates into the Eastern Region. The car will be rolled over and burned. But now Alan's adrenaline is flowing and Pam is acting like a coed from St. Mary's who just discovered a bar full of Notre Dame guys. She too is eager to explore the dark streets. There are no streetlights. This shocks the three of us. We expect light in a large city. We stumble through dark narrow streets and wonder if we'll ever find our way back to the Peace Corps hostel. We occasionally bump into dark figures in long flowing robes and visorless caps. A few Kanoites pass carrying small kerosene lamps to light the way. No one greets us.

We spot a dot of light far down a side street, walk to it, and enter. The bar is nearly devoid of furniture except for a few rickety card tables that wobble on the uneven cement floor. There is no bar, only a battered refrigerator full of quart bottles of Star beer. The only other customer is a military officer sitting at a back table with two prostitutes. The officer motions for us to join him. He is very drunk and the prostitutes are very bored. The officer laughs uproariously when he discovers we have been in the country only a few hours. "This is an Ibo bar," he explains. "You are in the *sabon gari*, the strangers' quarters. Do you understand?"

"Like a ghetto," I say. "You are a minority in Northern Nigeria."

The officer laughs again, the long loud laugh of the inebriate. "We are Christians from the East," he says. "You don't know about these things yet, but you'll learn soon enough. Many Ibos live in the North. We are businessmen. We make lots of money here. Like the Jews. We are like the Jews—rich, unwelcome strangers." He offers us drinks, the women. He offers to swap the two women for Pam. Everyone laughs except Pam. Even the prostitutes seem to find this funny. We decline the women and the swap but accept the drinks.

While we drink, the officer fondles the prostitutes and jokes with the barmaid, who is not in a joking mood. She wants to close up. We finish our drinks and rise to leave. The officer tries to detain us. "One day you must visit Eastern Nigeria," he says, his face glistening with sweat. "Ibo bars stay open all night. We are a happy people. Not like these Hausas. They are Muslim and don't drink. They don't know how to enjoy life. They are an ignorant people." He is very drunk and shakes our hands vigorously. "Will you still be in Kano this weekend?"

I explain that we will be leaving the next day.

"Too bad," he says. "You'll miss the fireworks at the palace."

"I don't understand," says Pam. "Is it a holiday?"

"A long holiday for the emir," says the officer. "The emir will never forget our fireworks. Well, good luck then. I am sure you will like Nigeria. We are a friendly nation," he says and again breaks into gales of laughter.

We return to the dark street and search in vain for another bar. We wonder about the Nigerian officer. We do not understand what he has told us. Now I know that he must have seen us as naive children, as people too ignorant to comprehend.

He has played a daring game with himself, with us—telling us his secret in cryptic terms that we brush off as inconsequential.

Maiduguri in Bornu Province is a medieval city, virtually unchanged for a thousand years. Crowds in long flowing robes and turbans still flow on foot through the bazaar as they always have. Goldsmiths still soften the metal with charcoal flames and still shape it with hand-held tongs and hammers. Tinsmiths still make cups and saucers, bowls and pails. Weavers weave on handmade wooden looms, and dyers dip the woven cloth into clay vats of dye (usually blue) that sit like so many puddles in an open courtyard. The dyed cloth dries on upended wicker baskets woven from reeds taken from the river shallows during the brief wet season. Blacksmiths still create swords, spears, and knives. Many other outmoded skills are still honored in Maiduguri.

The city is walled—the ramparts the only visible reminder of the Bornu Empire of the last century. The Kanuri people had conquered a vast area of sub-Saharan Africa before the British arrived with modern weapons—machine guns that mowed down charging cavalry and cannons that blew away mud walls. The Kanuri were forced to accept the might of the British Empire but otherwise chose with success to ignore the infidels. The Koran is still the source of values. The architecture is still African. The only visible signs of British presence are the English of street and stop signs and the stately neem trees that line boulevards. The British imported the trees from India.

The king's guards still walk the ramparts, watching the surrounding desert for marauders. The king is still there. He is called the *shehu*, the Kanuri word for an emir. The *shehu*'s palace dominates the city—the only multilevel building, containing dozens of rooms and enclosing its own courtyard. The courtyard is huge, with its own bazaar—fruit and vegetable sellers, a blacksmith shop, a tea shop (a concession to the British), a bakery, a leather merchant, and a radio repair. Many of the vendors are the wives, daughters, and sons of the *shehu*. How many wives does he have? No one seems to know. He has dozens of children, many of them students at my school.

In a place as isolated as Maiduguri, every white person in town comes out to the airport when a new white face is expected on the weekly flight. As I step off the plane they are all there—my fellow expatriates. The first to greet me are the two other Volunteers assigned to Bornu Teachers' College. Allen from California teaches Western Civilization remarkably well without a textbook, though one is on order from the previous year. Hard-working, intelligent, and close to his students, he is trying to learn Kanuri. Vic from California plays the guitar badly, plays basketball worse, but teaches math with humor and élan. He worries about everything—his health, his feet (he changes sneakers about once a month), the heat, life after Africa, life after death.

In the months ahead I will not see much of the other two Maiduguri Volunteers. Joe from New York is rumored to be working on some undefined community development project, but he spends every day from noon to midnight at the Lake Chad Club. JoMarie from New Jersey teaches sewing at the Girls' Technical Institute. She is fat, smelly, loud, and impractical. In the country only six months, she has already ruined two brand-new motorcycles by failing to remember to add oil. Now she is working on her third. She has a crush on her houseboy, complains incessantly about all things African, and eats every evening at the Club.

The Lake Chad Club is a hangover from colonial days—an all-white enclave in darkest Africa. Unless you're a waiter, bartender, dishwasher, groundskeeper, or some other kind of servant, you'd better be white or you'll never get through the front door. You won't even reach the door. The doorman will see to that. Most of the expatriates are members. Most, in fact, spend most of their waking hours there. Allen has never been inside. He detests the colonial mentality of the members. Vic goes there occasionally for a steak dinner and a movie. The steak dinner is the equivalent of about a quarter and the movie is free. I will go there sometimes with Vic on a Saturday night. At least once I will consume steak and chips and six double shots of rum and Coke, spending a grand total of about three dollars—the cheapest drunk I've ever had.

Also at the airport is a group of middle-aged elementary and high school teachers who have come to Africa under a program run by the University of Minnesota. They are conservative in politics and dress and pale in spite of the tropical sun. They all have leaves of absence from small-town Minnesota schools. They all have education degrees from second-rate Minnesota universities. They all believe wholeheartedly that life in a small town in Minnesota is superior to life anywhere else and that Midwestern American values of mom, apple pie, and shoot the commies are what everyone should have. They've read very few books, but they'd be in church on Sunday praying for victory in Vietnam if there were a church. Instead they go to the Club. Miss Dunn goes there to knit and to talk to the Club cats, feeding them bits of steak and a French fry or two from her plate. She is a spinster who still acts as if her students are Minnesota fourth-graders. Rob from Minneapolis plans on getting an Ed.D. in curriculum development when he returns to Minnesota. He is the only person in Maiduguri who always wears a suit. He has a pasty-faced matronly wife and five kids. He likes to talk about the internal dynamics of lesson plans and grammatical errors, especially dangling modifiers. A really good dangling modifier can set him howling for hours. He can conceive of nothing funnier. The Schmidts are just kind of pathetic. Mr. Schmidt is here to teach history but leaves that duty to Allen. Instead he sits at the Club every evening and gets quietly drunk on expensive scotch. His wife will have an affair with whoever is willing, but few are. Occasionally she traps some stranger in a corner and all but rapes him. The stranger is probably from so far out in the boondocks that he doesn't know about Mrs. Schmidt. It doesn't matter much anyway. Mr. Schmidt is usually oblivious. Sometimes he buys the guy a drink. Their son Dan has taken a year off from the university where he is studying physical education. He sleeps until noon, eats, and then appears every afternoon at four for basketball.

Basketball is a regular event. Male Peace Corps Volunteers and assorted other whites (a Greek, a couple of Lebanese, a Frenchman, a couple of Brits) play from four to five-thirty every day, including during the hot season when the temperature approaches 120 degrees and I sleep at night in the bathtub full of water. At our games the only spectator is Rosemary, a cute upper-class Brit with smoldering dark eyes and black hair. She has a terrific crush on Vic but he is too shy to do anything about it. A month after my arrival she will be bitten by a rabid bat on the leg, will become paralyzed on the left side from the shots, and will be flown back to England.

*   *   *

Bornu Teachers' College sits three miles outside the city of Maiduguri. The college is modeled on someone's idea of an English boys' boarding school from another era. The school has several blocks of classrooms, a staff room, a library containing moldy cheap editions of British literary classics of the nineteenth century and earlier, a science laboratory virtually empty of equipment, a block of dormitories for each form, and neat rows of staff bungalows.

A few bedraggled-looking flowers grow here and there along the foundations of staff bungalows, but otherwise there is no landscaping. The grounds blend without distinction into the semiarid plain.

My new home is a cement block dwelling with glass windows, tiled floors, mahogany furniture, electricity, a gas stove, a fridge, running water, and a flush toilet.

I am pleasantly surprised, for I have lived in much worse places in the States, particularly during my student days. I know that other Volunteers live in mud huts with no amenities, no water, no electricity. It's called going native. My new home is superior to the average Nigerian home to a ridiculous degree. I have more of everything—space, furnishings, plumbing. I do not complain. I feel only relief.

Before I even unpack I go off to meet the principal. If he were not a Nigerian, he would be straight out of a book about colonial life in the heyday of the British Empire. Mallam Hussein is in his walled garden with his wife. He is the only administrator to have such a garden. His house is also superior to the others—larger and more lavishly furnished. He is sipping a gimlet, surrounded by a gardener, a nanny for the baby, and a white-coated waiter. I realize immediately that servants are common, that all professionals in Nigeria have them. I will have one too.

This is strange. A few months ago I was a university student, poor and badgered, living in a roach-infested dump above a noisy bar and all-night pizzeria. Then I joined the Peace Corps to see how people in the Third World lived. Now I will have a servant who will call me "Suh" and who will not bristle at the title of houseboy, though I will. I will call him my steward; he will call his assistant his *small boy*.

The principal takes me around to meet the rest of the staff. Eighty percent are expatriates—from Britain, New Zealand, South Africa, Pakistan, India, and America. The Nigerian staff are Yoruba from the Western Region and a couple of Hausa from Kano. There are no Kanuri teachers, though the Kanuri are over ninety-five percent of the population of Bornu. Maiduguri is their capital. They do not like Hausa or Yoruba very much and detest Ibo.

Their hatred of the Ibo is economic. Over a million Ibo live in the North, several thousand in Maiduguri, where they own most of the small shops and all but one of the petrol stations. Ibos hold nearly all of the administrative positions in industry, banking, public utilities, and government. The Kanuri are left to do menial labor and subsistence and cash-crop farming (usually groundnuts). The reason for this economic disparity is simple: the Ibo are educated, the Kanuri are not.

Bornu Teachers' College has about 550 students. It is one of only three secondary schools in all of Bornu Province. The other two are the boys' secondary school with 400 students and the girls' sewing school with 150. Bornu has 3.5 million people.

One might wonder why there are so many schools in Ibo towns and villages in Eastern Nigeria and so few in Bornu. Again the answer is simple. Mass education is a threat to the traditional rulers of the North. An educated peasantry might not accept the medieval social structure of the North, with the emir and his family controlling wealth and politics. Also, the schools in the East are Christian mission schools, but the North is Muslim.

I wonder why I was sent here. I sense that I am being used, that I am cheap labor paid for by America. If I were not here, the Northern government would have to choose between hiring a Yoruba or Ibo or hiring a very expensive European. In a sense I am taking a job away from a Nigerian who is not wanted because of his tribe.

In some ways Bornu Teachers' College is Victorian. In a province where shops open around ten, close from two-thirty to four, and may or may not reopen later depending upon the mood of the shop owner, our students rise each school day between four-thirty and five, shower, and dress in identical uniforms—white button-down cotton shirts, dark blue cotton shorts, and sandals. Breakfast is served from five to six, followed by the morning assembly for announcements and prayers. Prefects take attendance and write up reports on missing boys. Then classes begin at twenty to seven.

All students take eight classes Monday through Friday, the last ending by two. The afternoons are used for siestas, sports, clubs, washing clothes, school maintenance. The evenings are filled by required study hall from six-thirty to eight-thirty. The boys are in bed and lights are out at nine. The campus grows quiet. Then at ten the city's generator goes off. All reading after that is done by kerosene lamp.

Saturdays begin at the same early hour, but classes end at noon. Then the students prepare the dormitories and classrooms for weekly inspection. Dormitories that fail the late afternoon inspection must repeat the clean-up process for reinspection. A second failure means a Sunday spent cutting grass, repairing buildings, and cleaning latrines while the other boys walk to town or play soccer or basketball.

*   *   *

In my English classes the students rise when I enter the room and stand by their desks until I indicate they should sit. When I call on someone, he rises, gives an answer, and sits down. Discipline problems are rare, for caning is common practice. A whip leans in the corner behind my desk, a reminder for the boys that they can be lashed for any serious breach of the rules. I do not cane, however. I learn quickly that the worst action I can take toward an offending student is to expel him from a lesson. He will beg to return, will plead for a caning or a work assignment instead. He is terrified of missing any lesson of the government-planned curriculum that prepares students for the West African Certificate Examination. To fail that exam is to fail school.

Names confuse me. Many are similar and are shortened to the same nickname. Abdul, Abdullahi, and Abdulkadir all become Abdul. Some names are simple reversals of others. Sometimes Abdul Musa decides to call himself Musa Abdul while Musa Abdul decides to call himself Abdul Musa. All this is maddening. Everyone has brown eyes, black hair, brown skin, identical uniforms. How am I to remember?

Students do all homework and classwork in booklets. Every day I either pick them up for correction or pass them back with a new assignment. Seventy booklets are picked up or returned each day. I hate the damned things. They rule my life, especially the evenings. They are piled across the far side of my dining table, one pile for each class. I correct while I eat, spilling gravy and bits of rice here and there on the pages. The students write in the margins and between the lines. This is their only paper, and they hoard it, make maximum use of it. I curse the piles, but they don't go away.

By midnight I am done. Then I make lesson plans for another hour. The walls of the room are spotted with large, flat, hairy brown spiders and yellow or green lizards. On each lampshade perches a three- or four-inch mantis. All of this wildlife is absolutely stationary unless an insect foolishly lands on a wall or circles too close to a shade. Then in a blur of motion almost too quick for the eye, the insect is caught and consumed. An instant later motionlessness has returned and I again forget about my menagerie.

At dawn I am awakened by sounds not usually associated with a college—roosters crow, chickens cackle, goats *ba,* babies cry, insects drone. Black beetles the size and weight of doorknobs whir and clank about my bedroom, bouncing again and again off the walls like maniacal mechanical toys. I crawl from under the heavy air inside the mosquito net and breathe in the cool air of dawn. After shaking my clothes clean of hidden scorpions and cockroaches and any other creepy or crawly things that might be there, I dress hurriedly in shorts, T-shirt, and sandals. In an hour it will be ninety degrees outside. Maman, the servant, has breakfast ready—toast, eggs from our own chickens (kept in a shed near his house), fried plaintain and tomatoes, melon.

Then I heft my two-foot stack of booklets and proceed to class. So goes the daily round.

The students come from small clusters of mud huts scattered like bits of chaff over the vast dry plain. In their thatch-roofed and earth-floored homes they have not eaten with knives, forks, and spoons. They have not lain on beds—simple straw mats have sufficed for them and the bugs. At Bornu Teachers' College they learn of silverware and beds for the first time. The daily events of their lives—their successes and failures, their births and deaths—remain as always in the inscrutable hands of Allah, that all-powerful and all-knowing deity who remains as much of a mystery as the mosquito nets, whose purpose only the white teachers comprehend.

* * *

My English classes have two texts—one a simple grammar and speller by a teacher in England who has never been to Africa; the other a reader, Ernest Hemingway's *The Old Man and the Sea*. When I protest, the department chairman tells me to make do. "They'll never learn anyway," he says. "Even the best of them never get anything quite right." The chairman is a bigoted and cynical New Zealander who has been out here since colonial days. He figures the choice of text is inconsequential.

I do not wish to teach a fishing story to students who have lived all their lives in the desert, who have never seen a body of water larger than a puddle in the rainy season. "Why did you order such a book?" I ask.

"Because it's short," the chairman replies, "and Hemingway uses simple words in simple sentences. Usually it takes an American education to be able to write like that. British writers are too sophisticated. We've got copies of Steinbeck's *The Pearl* too, but that's bloody awful."

"Why didn't you order a Nigerian novelist such as Chinua Achebe, Cyprian Ekwensi, or Wole Soyinka?" I ask.

"Don't be naive," says the New Zealander. "Achebe and Ekwensi are Ibos. These people hate Ibos. They'd rather kill them than read them. Soyinka is out because he's too damned difficult. He's so indecipherable he'll probably win the Nobel Prize someday."

"Then why not use a Muslim writer from the North?" I ask. "Surely they could relate to such a writer."

"There are no writers from the North," the chairman replies. "Not one."

* * *

Hemingway meets a classy breed in his Africa: Philip Percival, the white hunter; Baron von Blixen, the ex-husband of Danish writer Isak Dinesen; a Vanderbilt. He also travels in style under the care of Tanganyika Guides Ltd. Days consist of tracking game under the guidance of a professional hunter while African bearers carry the heavy guns, food, and drink. Evenings consist of warm baths in a portable tub, expensive whiskey by the fire, good fellowship. His is the mythic Africa that white men have sought with little success for four hundred years. Hemingway discovers the incredible beauty of East Africa—the rolling hills, the high plains brimming with animals. He shoots everything a white man is supposed to shoot when he's rich enough to be a world-class hunter: kudu, lion, rhino, waterbuck, eland, sable, buffalo, leopard, many kinds of bird, and more.

In the end Africa becomes the great misadventure of Hemingway's life, probably more debilitating than all his other wounds and accidents combined. Years later his African injuries will lead to migraines, to paranoia, and to the hallucinations that lead up to his suicide.

We in the Peace Corps call it WAWA, an acronym for West Africa Wins Again. Whenever a simple Stateside act becomes impossible in Nigeria, someone says WAWA, and everyone else nods in silent agreement. I don't know what Ernest called it. On his first safari he catches acute amoebic dysentery which leads to a prolapsed lower intestine. He has to leave the safari for doctoring in Nairobi. On his second trip he and his fourth wife, Mary (Pauline, his second wife, accompanies him on the first safari), are in two plane crashes. In the first Ernest sprains his shoulder; in the second he suffers a ruptured spleen, liver, and kidney, loss of vision and hearing, a crushed vertebra, paralysis of the sphincter, first-degree burns, and such a serious concussion that brain fluid soaks his pillow by morning.

Finally rescued from the bush, he falls into a fire he is trying to put out and suffers serious burns over much of his body.

There is more horror, but this will suffice. Needless to say, none of this is in any of Hemingway's African writings, including *Green Hills of Africa*. There the opening chapter consists of a bit of hunting, a wonderful literary conversation on the merits of classic American writers, and a lot of gimlets. The rains are approaching but I can still love the land he describes beatifically. I can chase those descriptions all the way to Maiduguri in Northern Nigeria. *Green Hills* is about the primordial hunt, about healthy competition among men, about Ernest's closeness to the land and to the people of the safari both white and African. He is a kind of Thoreau with a big-game rifle. His wives are seductive. He doesn't talk much about the heat, the insects, the fevers, the petty jealousies and arguments. He doesn't mention his brief fling with the Masai woman, Debba.

Instead he does what he does best—he describes in such a way that we long to be there. Or at least I do.

But I have Maiduguri in the hot season, with the harmattan blowing off the Sahara. The harmattan, that hot blast of furnace air that stings bare flesh and singes the hair, that coats everything with a fine even layer of red chalklike dust. Wipe it away and a new layer appears in seconds. There is no escape. The dust coats the mucus membrane of the nostrils, fills the ears, roughens the throat so that I spit and gag. The eyes redden and burn. Food is coated while it cooks, tastes of clay.

Outside the sun is a dull red eye and all horizons are obscured by a thick granular halo. Everything looks out of focus. People walk about with wet cloths covering mouths and nostrils. The cloths are red with dirt.

People stop speaking. Their throats feel like they've swallowed gravel. Students stop asking questions. They sit at their desks with their eyes closed and their minds far away where skies are blue again.

Hemingway writes much about war—about the ways it brings out both the worst and the best in people. But here in Nigeria the best is not evident in the soldiers who surround the homes of corrupt government leaders in the early morning hours of January 15 and execute these officials in their beds. Among the dead are the religious leader of the North, the Sardauna of Sokoto, and the Prime Minister of the Republic, Tafawa Balewa.

In May retaliatory mobs will swarm through Ibo quarters in Northern cities, burning and looting. They will chop thirty thousand men, women, and children to pieces with machetes.

All of this will become dead news, forgotten history rewritten by the victors, the Northern killers. The dead might just as well not have lived for all that the world will remember the violence of their passing.

I shall remain bitter. Twenty years later, at a dinner party in Michigan, I shall attack another guest, a Nigerian spouting the current theory that the Ibo leader Ojukwu is entirely to blame for the war. Nigerian atrocities will be conveniently forgotten.

After the attempted January coup, Allen, Vic, and I cluster about Allen's shortwave radio and wait for news. Radio Nigeria plays classical music hour after hour. All day the BBC tells us to stand by for an important bulletin, which doesn't come until the second day. Then we teachers huddle in the faculty lounge, discussing the loss of order, repeating again and again the little details that

suddenly have grown so important in our lives—who is dead,
who is missing, and who escaped; the names and tribe of assas-
sins; the personality of the Ibo Ironsi who has taken over as
Supreme Military Governor.

Ironsi appoints military governors for each region. In the East
he appoints Ojukwu; in the North Hassan Katsina.

Stories about both men abound, but thirty-two-year-old Ojukwu
is the more impressive. Son of one of the richest men in Nigeria,
he has had the best education money can buy—Epsom, Oxford,
Sandhurst. In England he has set a school record for throwing
the discus. He has a sharp mind and unquestioned courage, a
beautiful lawyer wife and two children.

After the May riots against Ibos in the North, he will quickly
prepare the densely populated East to accept up to one million
refugees. At the same time he will repatriate Northerners in the
East back to the North without reprisals.

In July he will survive the massacre of over two hundred Ibo
military officers by Northern soldiers. In that massacre Ironsi
will be shot, his body dumped into an unmarked grave in the
bush. Yakubu Gowon will seize power in Lagos.

After long negotiations Ojukwu will meet with Gowon at
Aburi, Ghana. Ojukwu will outmaneuver Gowon at every turn,
will get Gowon's promise to pay salaries to Ibos who have fled
from government posts in the North because their lives are in
danger. Later Gowon will renege on this and other promises.
More massacres will follow. Ibos will be driven into their own
small region, unable to enter the rest of Nigeria without endan-
gering their lives.

Ojukwu will lead his people to secession, to the birth of a new
nation, Biafra. He will give up his wealth and, eventually, his

chance to live at peace among his people. Great Britain, the Soviet Union, the United States all will support Nigeria. The British will supply tanks, artillery, and other field weaponry. The Soviets will supply MIGs and Egyptian pilots. The United States will build roads and will pressure its allies to respect Nigeria's blockade of Biafra. Nigeria has few ships to enforce the blockade on its own.

The world will assume the immediate collapse of Biafra, but it will not collapse yet. It has more Ph.D.s than the rest of black Africa put together and it will survive on its own initiative, its own ability to create a military economy with minimal outside aid.

But the vast military superiority of Nigeria will eventually overwhelm Biafran initiative, and the blockade will kill their children. Two million Biafrans will die, most of them children under ten. They will die of kwashiorkor, protein deficiency. Their bellies will swell to bursting, their limbs will shrink to sticks, their hair will turn red and fall out, and their eyes will grow dull and flat. They will die by the thousands every day near the end, too weak even to complain.

Like Kurtz, Ojukwu will see the horror. He will see it in the eyes of the dying children and of the children's mothers.

He will surrender command and fly off to ignominious exile in Europe. Biafra will be dead at two and a half. The war will end in January 1970, almost exactly three years after the initial coup that started the whole thing.

I will be in California by then, surrounded by crazy hippies and flower children who think a new American revolution is just around the corner. When they say that, I ask them if they have been to Dubuque lately. The death of Biafra will bring back memories of Robert Kennedy, of King, of JFK. I will cry.

*   *   *

In January 1967 this is the going price for a houseboy in Nigerian pounds (one pound equals $2.80):

> In a Nigerian household—4 pounds
> In an Indian household—4.5 pounds
> In a British household—6 pounds
> In an American household—7 to 10 pounds

Needless to say, American householders are very popular in Nigeria.

To be my houseboy, I hire Mamman Jos, a stocky middle-aged man with a pleasant and fatherly manner. Mamman, his wife, and a small son live in a single-room servant's quarters behind my bungalow. I myself am a kind of king by Nigerian standards, with a small kitchen, a dining room, a bedroom, and a bathroom with shower and tub. Mamman cleans, cooks, washes clothes, and shops for groceries.

I am ecstatically happy that Mamman does the shopping, for the favorite exercise of all Nigerians is bargaining for a sale. They are fierce bargainers, the shopping equivalent of Gurkha assault troops. It doesn't matter what they are trying to sell, just as long as there is an opportunity for profit. Nigerians prefer to bargain with foreigners, especially Americans, for we are a potential source of lucrative profit. Northern Nigerians put faith in Allah and in the knowledge that all Americans are wealthy, that they all are perfectly willing after a little coercion to throw vast sums of money at a Nigerian in return for the most inconsequential and worthless of items. In addition, Americans are a potential source of stories. Nigerians love to collect "gullible American" stories the way some Americans love to collect "dumb

Polack" jokes. When I'm bargaining with a Nigerian, I can see the delight in his eyes. Those eyes say, "Soon I will be rich and soon this American will say or do something really stupid, and tonight my friends and I will laugh about it. My wife will laugh about it. My children will laugh. Even the baby will laugh."

I know from Peace Corps training that I must bargain for everything in Nigeria—food, clothes, a taxi, furniture, a haircut, the use of a toilet when I am away from home and there is not a bush in sight. Everything.

I also know that Nigerians will always begin the bargaining process by offering an object at approximately twice its actual value. Then I must make an offer of half its value. Then he comes down a little and I go up a little and so on. Anywhere from a half hour to two days later, a deal is struck.

Allen and Vic assure me that this is the process. Still, when I make my first venture into the world of Nigerian capitalism, I am ripped off. I return from the market after a half hour of vociferous bargaining for a wooden carving of a Fulani herdsboy. I happily show my purchase to Allen. He already owns several identical heads. He asks me what I paid. I tell him. He breaks into gales of laughter. He rolls on the floor, holding his sides. "What's so funny?" I say.

"The price you paid," he says.

"Then how much did you pay for yours?" I ask.

"I won't tell you," he says. "It'll only piss you off."

Eventually I learn to bargain reasonably well; that is, I will be as successful as most other foreigners and better than some. That will be a necessity. The Peace Corps will pay me only one hundred and twenty-five dollars a month.

I will become a successful bargainer by not really giving a damn whether or not I buy the coveted object. After all, why in hell do I need a wooden carving or a leather pouf? I'd rather have a new baseball or a hockey puck. I will be approached by a Nigerian and I will say, "I don't want that!" He will then offer a lower price. I will begin to walk away. He will again lower the price, this time drastically. This means he is now offering the object at somewhere close to double its value, common practice. Now we can begin to bargain fairly. Still, I know I will lose. I don't care. I only want to be able to keep my dignity, to prevent the Nigerian shop owner from breaking into gales of laughter, to prevent other Nigerians from running from everywhere to see the fool bargain. I hate that. Eventually it no longer happens. I have learned.

The students are also wonderful bargainers. They quibble over every error marked on every paper. They erase grades and insist I have made a mistake. They strike bargains with the best students and get them to write all of the class's essays. They question my knowledge of grammar and insist that American English is not the same as Nigerian English. They try to extend the date for completed assignments. They turn in phony doctors' reports by the basketful. They write their own excuses and assume, against all school policy, that these are acceptable. Here is a sample:

My Dear Mr. L. Anderson.
Today I'm not feeling good I have trouble stomach age and head age.
I'm serious I'm not fooling you. Mr. L. Anderson
Adamu Dala

Or this, from a student who caught gonorrhea from a prostitute:

My Master Mr. L. A. his eminence
I'm very sorry that I'm going to miss classes today, it's not because I'm lazy, but the reason is this.

Last night I couldn't sleep because of my sickless. I have very sore penis. Sir, you know what I mean.

Thank's B.M.

At the Lake Chad Club bar I sit down beside an English banker recently transferred from Lagos to the local Barclay's branch. The banker is about fifty, very proper in a stuffy sort of way, and has strong views on everything and everybody, especially Americans. "It's refreshing to meet an American who isn't a damned fool," he says to me by way of introduction, all the time shaking my hand vigorously. How he has instantly arrived at the conclusion that I'm not a damned fool is beyond me, since we've never met before. "Maybe young people like you will one day be able to change the American outlook towards the world," he adds. "I'd like to be able to tell you I've seen a change, but it wouldn't be true. No, I'd have to say Americans are just as big fools now as they were during the war. That was my first contact with the Yanks. I remember how struck I was at first by all the glamour of their army—their peanuts and popcorn machines, their showers and portable toilets. It astounded me. Then I began to think, What are they going to use for ammunition, peanuts and popcorn? They were just too damned arrogant with all their gloss and their shiny shoes. Fortunately for the Allies they didn't come into the war until forty-one or they'd've made a hell of a mess. And I'll tell you right now that they're going to make a hell of a mess of this African thing, too, if they don't change their ways. Look how they treat the people here! This organization of yours, for example. Peace Corps they call it. Peace hell!"

"How do you know I'm a Peace Corps Volunteer?" I ask. "We've only just met."

"Well, look at you!" says the banker. "You're wearing those bloody cut-off shorts with loose threads hanging everywhere, a

T-shirt that advertises a brand of American beer and that looks like you've been wearing it for ten years, a bloody cricket hat . . . what do you call it across the Atlantic? Baseball, is it? . . . and those silly leather sandals from the local market. No self-respecting European would wear such an outfit! No American would either, except Peace Corps."

"You've got us there," I say. "We are a bit informal."

"Worse than that," says the banker. "Your bunch causes more trouble here than your AID's and USIS's combined. You just don't know a thing about diplomacy. What do they call you back in the States—the kiddie corps? I've been watching your organization in action. You ignore us British completely and go your own arrogant way, and who else is important here except the Europeans?"

"What's so wrong with that?" I ask. "After all, this is Nigeria, not Britain. In their country we need to get along with Nigerians."

"Nigerians!" exclaims the banker. "That's the trouble with you Americans. You play palsy-walsy with these damned blacks as if you cared. Sure they say they like you. They like your money, that's what they like. Americans are just too gullible. These blacks don't like any white man. Look what they say when they make such a mess out of their own bloody country. They blame it on the British. They chop each other up with machetes and then they say it's our fault, that we didn't prepare them for independence. It wasn't our idea to give them independence now, was it? Who killed all the Ibos anyway? The British or the Hausa? If it had been up to the British they wouldn't be chopping each other up, that's for sure, because Nigeria would still be the Queen's colony with the Queen's troops in Kano. Imagine giving independence to this uncivilized pack of pagans! That was an American move, you know. They were afraid a few ignorant natives wouldn't like them if they didn't go along with the UN, so they pushed this independence bill through the General Assembly. I hope they see their mistake now. You can't let these people go it alone. It's like taking the mother away from the baby.

"As a banker, I'll tell you another thing—you can't trust these people with money. They have no morals. They'll rob you blind if you give them a chance. The best thing is not to let them have the opportunity. When one of these guys with his kooky-looking robes comes strolling arrogantly up to my desk, pulls out a cigar, and says he'd like two thousand, I let him have two hundred. If he protests I tell him I'll count to three, and if he hasn't said yes by then, he'll get nothing. They always say yes, of course. If I let them have too much money, they'll probably use it against us. Get enough of these damned blacks rich and they'll throw you out of their filthy country. Not that I care because I'll have my bundle. There is money to be made here."

A month after my arrival, at the end of Ramadan, the streets are filled with the *shehu*'s knights. These blue-robed gentlemen gallop everywhere on brightly caparisoned steeds. At the end of the day they rush in equestrian lines up to the outer walls of the palace, wheeling their horses in clouds of thick red dust and waving their swords and spears in the air. They shout their allegiance to the *shehu* in Kanuri and their allegiance to God in Arabic. The *shehu* is a shriveled old man sitting on an elaborately carved wooden throne on the flat roof of the palace. He is surrounded by attendants. One holds an umbrella over his head to protect him from the sun. Another fans him. A third chases mosquitoes away with a horsetail whisk. The *shehu* faces his army below but otherwise ignores the commotion. He looks very tired.

I am observing this pageantry with the other two Volunteers from my school. One of them has a telescopic lens on his camera.

He focuses it on the *shehu* and laughs. He lets me look and I laugh too. The *shehu* has fallen asleep.

Afternoons I coach the basketball team. Our concrete court is outside, without walls or roof. Waves of heat shimmer off the surface. My team is tall, rough on opponents, and only occasionally clumsy and unorthodox. During Ramadan they play hard while fasting—no food or drink from dawn to dusk, even their spittle not swallowed.

The hoops are on metal poles too hot to touch. The backboards are wire mesh to let the harmattan wind pass through. The ball strikes the mesh, the mesh gives, the ball drops straight down and through the hoop. I teach the boys an American jump shot. It doesn't matter how hard they shoot. The ball still drops straight down off the backboard. I teach them an overhead fastball, the good old high, hard one. The ball slams into the backboard, drops straight down and through.

We reach the Provincial finals by beating a series of teams on our own court. We travel to Yola by truck for the championship game. It's difficult to tell which the road contains more of, pavement or hole. In Arizona some of the potholes could be mistaken for the Grand Canyon. In the cab Dan from Minnesota and I constantly bounce from the seat to the ceiling, alternately striking our heads and butts. In the open bed the players clutch the sides desperately. To avoid this ocean of potholes we pull off the pavement altogether and drive along the dust-choked shoulder. A red cloud boils beneath us and out behind. Soon it seeps in through every crack until we can hardly see the dash. The road has disappeared. The team in back is coughing and hacking and pounding on the cab roof, pleading to return to the pavement.

We do and bounce onward, our truck a kind of pogo stick with wheels. "Some of these potholes must be small lakes in the wet season," says Dan. "Probably full of crocodiles and hippos, with ducks floating on the surface."

We arrive at Yola Training College. Their court has hardwood backboards. My team slams the ball off the wood as if it were wire mesh. In practice they crack one of the boards. In the game their shots carom off as if shot from catapults. I call time and tell them to forget the backboard, to shoot only for the rim. In the second half they come from a dozen points down to win the championship by six.

We celebrate the victory a week later by roasting an entire dressed goat over a bed of coals.

In Northern Nigeria I am lonelier than I will ever be again. I am cut off from family, community, and country. There are no newspapers, no television, no stereo, few books. There is no easy way to meet Kanuri men, for the Peace Corps has taught me the Hausa language but not Kanuri. The Kanuri live in isolated compounds separate from us and from each other.

Kanuri compounds are surrounded by high walls, with broken glass embedded in the top to keep out trespassers. The master lives in the only house with an entrance to the outside. His wives and children live in perpetual isolation in other homes tucked into corners of the courtyard. All Kanuri women spend their lives in such a closed space, rarely if ever venturing outside. For a white man Maiduguri is a city of men. I feel like I am in purdah myself, cut off from the female half of the world's population.

I write long letters to Tanya. We plan to wed in July.

I will be haunted by Africa, by what it will create. Africa is the beginning of my life after Maine, of my life with Tanya. I will become husband and father in Africa, will begin twenty years of mistakes. Or maybe it will be one long, long mistake, an elaborate mesh ensnaring Tanya and me and our son. We will tear at each other, rend the threads of experience. In the end we will go our separate ways, dead to each other in physical presence, alive always inside where the memories linger on and on and the pain can only grow.

Today a camel train passes through the college campus, the animals laden with great brown sacks. The four men of the train are Tuaregs, dressed in layers of loose blue cotton from their turbans to their ankles. Only their eyes show—eyes that burn with the fierceness of desert distances and with the arrogance that all nomads hold for settled folk such as I. The Tuaregs say nothing. I feel like a spectator at a movie set.

It is May 29, 1967. In Kano ninety-two Ibos have been killed, their markets and homes ransacked and burned. Many more have died in Jos, Kaduna, Zaria, Katsina, with riots and killing on a lesser scale in smaller places. I sit on the front porch getting my haircut from the Ibo gentleman who pedals his bike out from the town once a month to trim European heads. A series of lorries roar by, heading away from Maiduguri at a mad pace. The barber realizes immediately that the lorries are loaded with people. Suspecting the worst, he runs out into the road and hails a lorry, which pulls onto the shoulder in a cloud of red dust. The barber learns the Ibos are leaving for the bush and safe refuge from rioting which has broken out all over town. Two of the barber's friends are in the bed of the lorry, along with about thirty other people. The barber's friends inform him that his shop has been pillaged and burned, that his family has already fled. There is nothing for him to do but to join the refugees. Just then a mob of my students rushes past my house. They are shouting curses and brandishing machetes and stones. My barber is pulled hurriedly into the lorry bed and the vehicle pulls away, gears whining. The students hurl several stones that fall short of the fleeing truck.

Halfheartedly the students return to my house and try to take the barber's Chinese-built bicycle, which leans against the wall by my kitchen door. I argue with them. They relent and I put the bike inside until the barber can reclaim it. He never will.

I remain with half a haircut until the following day, when Vic finishes the job.

For several days unsubstantiated rumors have swept the town. Apparently the police, acting on a tip, sliced open the bags of gari (corn meal) arriving by lorry two days ago and discovered a machine gun with a thousand rounds as well as numerous small arms. Then a tale swept the town that the Ibos, who are the comptrollers of the baking industry, had poisoned all the bread the Kanuri were eating. A mob attacked and destroyed Ibo shops and homes. Most Ibos are now hiding in the bush; a few others are besieged in churches and police barracks.

The police are not much protection. For example, a gang of Kanuri entered an Ibo hotel and began to beat an adolescent who worked there. The proprietor, a shrunken eighty-five-year-old Ibo man, protested while his Kanuri friend, a policeman, looked on. The mob turned on the old man and beat him nearly to death. Then his friend of over a quarter century arrested him for disturbing the peace and inciting a riot. The old man is now in the hospital but is not expected to survive. Kanuri are searching the hospital for Ibos and are macheteing them in their beds.

I learn this from Charlie, a Yale-educated crackerbarrel Vermonter who is staying at my house recovering from a combination of malaria and hepatitis. Charlie had been walking around the world when he collapsed this morning in the road in front of the college. Mr. Schmidt found him sprawled in the center of the road, unconscious, with a heavy pack on his back and his head bare under that terrible sun. Mr. Schmidt brought Charlie to my house, where I covered him with ice packs to cool him down until the doctor arrived. The doctor verified that Charlie had heatstroke aggravated by mild malaria and mild hepatitis. Charlie is resting here for a couple of days.

Charlie was in the market when the riots broke out, was staying in the Ibo hotel when the proprietor was beaten. He decided to leave Maiduguri, to walk to northern Cameroons. That's when he collapsed.

Charlie is an amazingly self-sufficient and self-possessed guy, but even he is worried about where he will go from here. He knows that after the Cameroons he will have to cross Chad, and there is civil war there. Beyond Chad is Sudan and another war and beyond that Ethiopia and another war. We make a list. Today there are civil wars in the previously named plus Burundi, Rwanda, Rhodesia, South Africa, Angola, Mozambique, Fernando Po, Cameroons, Gabon, Mauritania, Spanish Sahara, Dahomey, Togo—and that's only the African list. It doesn't include all the mayhem in Asia and Latin America.

Charlie and I talk about Americans and how blissfully ignorant they are of all this. We wonder if King will wake them up. Or will Robert Kennedy?

*   *   *

Today sunblistered corpses steam like melting butter under a torrid sun in all of the cities and towns of the North. Yet the country holds together. In America the latest mass killer has climbed a Texas tower to shoot over twenty students in Austin. My nerves are raw. I want to *do* sosmething about all this carnage. Instead, I drink rum and Coke at the bar of the Lake Chad Club. I hear the thump of the tennis balls, hear the splashing from the pool as the white bodies cool. White shorts glisten in the reflected light of the pool deck. Lean tanned bodies stretch about the pool on lounge chairs under canvas umbrellas. A couple of young minds are loudly discussing a James Bond novel. Everybody else is engrossed in the dull quiet passage of the hours.

The bar is busy. Outside, people raze and loot and scream *Allah! Allah!* as blades fall too swiftly into soft terrified necks. There is an old colonial at the bar, a Britisher, cynical and bitter. "I say, 'Chop 'em good, boys,' " he says. "The bloody little bastards! Never do a thing we tell 'em! Insolent! That's what they are! Damned Ibos! Wouldn't have one in the house myself. Give me a Hausa or a Kanuri every time. I snap my finger, he jumps. Way they ought to be."

The colonial takes a long drink and snaps his finger. The bartender comes out of his reverie long enough to pour him another. All around the bar people nod at each other, agree that things have turned nasty. They wonder if it will affect banking, if they'll be able to cash their checks as usual on Friday. More bodies splash in the pool. Two Nigerian women watch through a crack in the fence. An attendant chases them away.

June is the cruelest month, the heart of the hot season. The harmattan has stopped blowing. The land bakes in a great stillness as if it were irretrievably and eternally dead, as if the last vestige of life has fled beneath the steady pummeling of the sun. In early afternoon the temperature hovers between 118 and 125 degrees. Gradually through the night it drops into the nineties, but thirty minutes after sun-up it's over 100 again. School is virtually impossible. I eat and sleep in the bathtub.

One afternoon I sit alone on my porch, trying to catch a breeze. With an orange squash in my hand, I stretch my feet comfortably over the railing and wonder if I can avoid getting a burn if I stay in the shade. An overloaded lorry approaching from the west suddenly begins to belch black smoke. It backfires, stalls, and rolls to a stop on the stretch of road right in front of me.

The driver climbs down, wraps his hands in strips of cloth before he touches the hot metal, and opens the hood. A cloud of oily steam hisses out. When it dissipates the driver searches the bowels of the engine for the problem. He pops his head out to call his assistant, who brings him a broad-brimmed straw hat.

The bed of the lorry is full of refugees, schoolgirls still in the classroom uniforms they were wearing when they fled. They climb stiffly down from the open back of the lorry. They try to make themselves presentable by straightening their blue skirts and tugging at their white blouses. Clouds of red dust nearly obscure them from view as they stamp their feet to ease the cramps and stiffness of standing in a moving lorry for five hundred miles.

A tall commanding girl converses with her friends briefly, pointing in my direction. Then she shyly approaches. She carries nothing but a schoolbook, looks exhausted and filthy. Her voice is cracked from heat and dehydration, her lips are swollen and blistered. "Do you have water, suh?" she asks in a barely audible whisper.

"I'll get you some," I say. "I'll be right back."

Inside, from the coolness of the refrigerator, I collect all the bottles of water. There are five. I bring them out to the porch.

By now all the girls have gathered in the inviting shade of the porch. They are no longer shy. They have scattered themselves in small groups and are talking in low tones. I pass out the water bottles and return to the interior of the house for glasses, but before I return the girls have drained every bottle.

"Where are you coming from?" I ask.

"Kano," several reply at once.

"Where are you going?" I ask.

"To the East," they all say together. The tall girl explains that they are Ibos, that their school was attacked by a mob and some of their friends killed. They don't know where their parents are but presume that they are in other lorries also traveling to the East. This lorry with an open bed, the Nigerian version of a bus, picked up the girls at their school as the mob burned it and killed the staff, four Catholic sisters.

"And what will you do when you get to the East?" I ask. "Do you have homes? Will you stay with relatives?"

"We will fight!" a girl replies quickly.

"We will make a nation!" another girl exclaims.

"You left Kano with nothing?" I ask.

The girls do not reply. They are beginning to show just how tired they are. Several collapse onto the porch floor and close their eyes. The tall girl tells me they are going into the Cameroons. Then they will travel south to the coast and reenter Nigeria in the Eastern Region, in Iboland. "It's too dangerous to travel south of Kano," she says. "Soldiers set up roadblocks and shoot everyone."

"So you've had to travel hundreds of miles out of your path."

As the girls rest, I watch the road. A convoy of a dozen lorries swirls by in clouds of red dust. All are packed with children.

Truckloads of children.

The driver shouts from the roadside. He has repaired the lorry and is ready to push on.

"We will go now," says the girl who first approached me. "We have no money for the water."

"Water is free."

"No," she says. "Ibos pay their way. Take this book for your kindness."

"But I don't need it. You do," I say.

"Not anymore," she says with a downcast look of her eyes. "The school is burned. The Catholic sisters are dead. Now I will be a fighter!" She gives me her dust-laden and frayed copy of *The Old Man and the Sea*. On the inside cover she had neatly penned her name and class: Flora Nwobi, Form One. On the opposing page is stenciled "St. Theresa's Catholic School for Girls, Kano."

The girls filter out to the road, climb heavily into the lorry bed. As the driver veers his vehicle back onto the road, they wave good-bye through the dust. "We love Ojukwu," they shout in unison. "We will win."

I am correcting papers in the bathtub, lying in four inches of cool water while outside the earth bakes in 118 degrees. Something heavy thumps against the wall. Then a series of solid thumps sets my adrenaline flowing. I throw on shorts and sandals and hurry outside. A herd of long-necked Fulani cattle has surrounded my house. It's a small herd—maybe fifty animals. They are languid—have already eaten the few half-dead plants by my kitchen door. They have left many steaming patties in the red earth I call my front yard. The herdsboy is sitting in a narrow line of shade by the side of the building. He's maybe ten years old, with a long stave in his hand and wearing a wide-brimmed straw hat, sandals cut from a tire, and a kind of rough toga draped over one shoulder and falling to his knees. He's a handsome lad seemingly indifferent to the location of his herd or the sudden appearance of a white man. I say hello in Hausa but he says nothing, does not acknowledge my presence. I go inside and return with a bottle of water. He drinks thirstily, still sitting, staring off at the horizon which shimmers in the heat. When the bottle is empty he leaves it on the ground in the shade, rises, and walks away in long slow strides. I watch until he and his cattle are flickering dots in the desert.

Tanya will try to mold our son into the kind of man all of her feminist books and magazines have told her is the ideal male. She will insist that he have no violent toys, play no violent games, own no violent comics or books, see no violent movies, use no violent language.

She will try to teach him French at an early age, will later insist that he study it in school. She will buy him expensive and beautiful coloring books of medieval tapestries and Hopi kachinas. She will try to implant in him the kinds of interests that she believes will make him sensitive to the interests and needs of women.

When our son is old enough to reach the keys, he must have piano lessons. He will not be enthusiastic. At his recital he will fall asleep. At first she will think he is faking, but no—he will be sound asleep.

The lessons will continue until our son is in the seventh grade. That year his mother will insist that he join the choir. He will resist. She will become adamant. He will lose temporarily, but as the only male member, he will tear up the scores and shoot spitballs at the choirmaster. He will leave the choir, quit the piano lessons, never touch a keyboard again.

In high school she will buy him a soccer ball and cross-country skis, but he will play football and baseball and do alpine skiing. He will upset the French teacher by writing obscene dialogues in his workbook. She will insist that he dress in proper attire but he will only wear T-shirts emblazoned BLACK SABBATH, THE DEAD KENNEDYS, or HARLEY DAVIDSON. He will listen to very loud hard rock, will collect Conan the Conqueror comics which she will tear up because of their portrayal of women. She will buy him novels by well-known women writers and by men that her feminist books approve of, but he will read science fiction, Bukowski, Mailer, and Hunter Thompson. She will insist he accompany her to foreign films, but he will go alone to see *First Blood, Aliens, Friday the 13th,* and anything else violent and frightening and clichéd.

Our son will wreck his knee in the last football game of his senior year. She will say she's glad, that he deserves the pain and disablement for choosing such a sport, that I am to blame for letting him play.

Our son will have a string of girlfriends in high school and college, will break up with all of them. She will say he deserves his miseries, that no woman could possibly put up with him, with his cold and withdrawn and aberrant personality.

Our son will be brilliant, will get A's without ever studying, will win a National Merit Scholarship, will have his choice of colleges. He will leave for the university at eighteen, will begin the study of philosophy and literature. Now left to his own devices, he will discover Shakespeare and theater, the German philosophers, Turkish. He will come home for that first Christmas. His mother will try one last time to manipulate him, to make choices for him. She will tell him how to act around women and around her friends, how he must change if he ever wants to be happy. She will tell him what he ought to watch on

TV, what movies he ought to avoid. When he is packing to return to school, she will insist he take a suitcoat and expensive button-down shirts. She will insist he take a heavy winter coat.

He will rebel, will rip the shirts in half, will tell her what he thinks of her past indiscretions, her numerous attempts to govern his character and personality. His anger will burst out in the form of a long monologue full of pain and suffering.

Then he will step out of our lives, will return to school, will never come home again. He will go his separate way, always finding summer work in another state, always finding a friend to visit during vacations.

He will be lost, alone in America.

Like me. Like Tanya.

A crazy woman comes into my classroom. She stands just inside the doorway, her eyes rolling wildly and deep stifled moans issuing from purple lips. I have a devil of a time getting rid of her. The Nigerians won't touch her. They say they'll go crazy within three days if they do. They say she must have made an oath on the Koran which was a lie, that her insanity is a punishment from Allah.

Today is a Sunday. I rise early and go with Allen to visit the goldsmith who is making the wedding rings out of a Victorian gold sovereign. We spend the day and the early evening at the shop, watching the goldsmith soften the coin with the aid of a charcoal fire and a hand-held bellows. The malleable gold is gradually stretched into strands no thicker than horsehair. Then the strands are woven into the rings. After the process is finished, Allen and I go to an Indian movie.

The cinema has walls but no roof. The chairs are benches without backs. The screen is a whitewashed high wall that causes a glare in the image. The audience cannot understand Hindi and neither can we, but everyone hoots and hollers at the constant stream of jujitsu, karate, dancing girls, fist fights, sword fights, flying carpets, weaving snakes, and daredevil leaps. "I've seen half a dozen of these things and I still can't detect a plot," says Allen.

I return about midnight to discover my steward has been arrested as a thief and is in jail. Mamman's wife is hysterical. She has been frantically waiting for my return, urges me to go immediately to the police station to retrieve her husband. In my absence Mamman discovered someone had broken into my house by removing the glass from a window. The thief took all my clothes, a typewriter, and the Ibo barber's bicycle. When Mamman bicycled immediately into town to report the theft to the police, he was arrested.

Allen and I dash to the police station on Allen's motorcycle. The two policemen on duty insist that Mamman or one of his friends did the robbery. I don't believe them. We argue. I plead for Mamman's release, tell them that I will not press charges. It doesn't matter.

I pay the police a dash of five pounds. They immediately release Mamman. He is subdued, terrified he has lost his job. I assure him that everything is okay, that I don't believe he did it. The next day, to make him feel better, I give Mamman money for a movie, an old American serial from the forties with the hero left in peril again and again until the final reel. He loves the film and asks for extra money the next night so he and a friend can go again. I pay for both.

A couple of days later Mamman has grown sullen. He mopes through his work, indicates it is my fault that he was arrested, that I should not have been so careless as to leave my possessions unprotected inside my house while I was gone. He asks for a raise. Because of the circumstances I refuse. He gets the money anyway by begging for an advance for some new sandals, for medicine for a sick child, for a new wrapper for his wife.

I take my problem to Allen, who has already hired and fired several servants. "This is crazy," I explain. "I'm the one who was robbed and I'm being treated like the villain. Why did I give him the money? Why should I feel guilty?"

"WAWA," says Allen matter-of-factly. "West Africa Wins Again."

Thieves tried to break into Mallam Hussein's house last night while he was watching *Zorro* at the cinema and his wife was visiting a female friend in the town. Hussein's Hausa wife had planted a thief-preventive plant all around the house. The thieves brought a spade and, being careful not to touch anything but the soil around the plant, began to dig all of them up and pile them away from the house so they could enter. After several hours and still many plants to go, the thieves gave up. This plant is about six inches high and resembles a lily.

In class several students wore capes and masks. *Zorro* has created a kind of carnival atmosphere.

Students bring me a Chinese propaganda photo magazine about the war in Vietnam. It is titled *Liberated Peoples Will Triumph—U.S. Aggressor Will Be Defeated, No. 3.* I love that *No. 3.* The market is full of this kind of magazine. This particular one uses pictures from *Life* but with different captions. In *Life* the caption below a picture of an exhausted and stressed-out helicopter pilot says that he has made two unsuccessful attempts to retrieve a friend left behind after a firefight. The Chinese caption says the pilot is overcome by remorse after a day of murdering innocent women and children.

The students want to know why America is attacking Vietnam. I try to explain. Mostly the students want to know how we are profiting from the war. They know that the British profited by colonizing Nigeria, that the British are still profiting. I tell them that the war is costing America millions of dollars per day, that Vietnam has no resources or products that America can use. The students are shocked. "Either you are lying, sir, or Americans are very stupid," says Abdulkadir, a Form Five student with a lot of common sense.

More Ibos have been murdered in Katsina after a rumor that Colonel Hassan, the military ruler of the North, was imprisoned in Lagos by Ibo officers. The rumor says Hassan made himself invisible by juju, escaped from jail, and flew in the fashion of Captain Marvel to the North. Students say Hassan has called for the death of Ibos, that radio broadcasts in Hausa call Ibos cannibals who eat Hausa children.

I have a pile of aerograms purchased at the post office. Nearly every day I mail an aerogram to Tanya with news and love. Today in the midst of a sandstorm the post office truck comes out to the college to deliver a terse message from Tanya, three lines written on a postcard. She is angry, wants to know why I have not written for a month and why I have never responded to a telegram she sent three weeks earlier. The telegram never arrived.

I take the letter to Mallam Hussein and ask him what's going on. He acts surprised. "I assumed you knew about the fire truck," he says.

"What fire truck?"

"The one at the airport. It's out of commission—the water pump is shot. Until it's repaired, there are no flights."

"How long has this been going on?"

"No flights for over a month. You could inform your friend of the problem by overland mail, but overland mail usually takes weeks and it probably would not arrive until after your wedding."

"How long before they repair the fire truck and resume flights?"

"Last time it took six months."

I am downcast. I go to the post office to ask the postmaster to send all my previous letters overland, but he refuses. "You have paid extra for airmail service," he says, "and we must give you that service."

"But there is no airplane," I argue. "My mail has been sitting in a mailbag right here for weeks."

"When the plane comes, we will send it," he says.

"Can I have the letters back so I can change the postage?"

"Once the mail is in our charge, no one may interfere," he says in a commanding voice.

"But the plane may not come for weeks. Who knows when they will get the parts to repair the fire truck."

"It's in Allah's hands," he replies.

I leave the post office to visit Maiduguri's only stationery store, but it was owned by an Ibo and has been burned. I ask for letter envelopes in several other shops but am told there are no longer any envelopes since the riots. In frustration I write my latest letter on an aerogram. On the outside after I seal it I write DON'T SEND THIS AEROGRAM BY AIR.

At the post office the postmaster tells me my message is absurd, that of course they will send my aerogram by air, for I have paid two extra pence for this privilege.

Standing erect and trying to speak in the most commanding voice I can muster, I say, "Sir, there is no plane," and he says I should have thought of that before using an aerogram.

"You have entrusted this letter to us," he says. "We must do this up right. Besides, one day there will be a plane. Then your letter will be in Lagos in only five hours. Unless of course the plane crashes again."

"I beg of you to send my letter overland." I am now pleading with this man though I would prefer to strangle him with the official post office tie he wears with such overwhelming dignity and pride.

"But we are servants of the people," he says, pugnaciously puffing out his chest. "We mustn't waste the people's money. Besides, thousands of Nigerians would love to send their letters by airmail, but they can't afford it."

I decide to give up on the aerogram. I will write another letter and give it to Tanya in person when I see her.

Since the troubles began, the students have been buying powerful juju charms in the market. This juju is supposed to protect them from knives and bullets. If someone shoots at them, the juju will cause the bullet to fall at their feet. The students carry the juju in small leather pouches and hang these from string necklaces inside their shirts. They have to hide the juju from the Muslim teachers or they will be severely punished.

Around noon Vic returns from the market with the same kind of juju. He carries the little leather pouch in his shorts pocket. In the faculty lounge he brings it out to show me. He says he is amazed at its price and wonders how the students can afford it. He thinks it will be a wonderful conversation piece when he returns to the States. We make jokes about its power and bat it back and forth a couple of times with the flats of our hands as if it were a tennis ball. One of the Nigerian teachers notices it and becomes incensed. "Why do you have that juju? Don't you know that it doesn't work? You have wasted your money!"

Vic smiles sheepishly, blushes, and tries to hand the juju to the Nigerian, but he refuses to touch it. He is very offended and says we are ridiculing his religion. Vic tries to explain that he doesn't believe in juju, that he bought it as a joke, but the Nigerian colleague insists on proving that juju doesn't work. We try to explain that such proof is not necessary, but the Nigerian will not listen. He insists that we accompany him to his home nearby where we wait in the yard while he gets his dane-gun, a locally made shotgun that shoots whatever is wadded into the bore— nails, bolts, bearings, bits of iron.

Joining us in the yard our colleague catches one of the many chickens pecking for stray insects in the narrow band of shade at the side of the house. He ties the juju around the chicken's neck with a bit of string and then releases the bird, which immediately retreats to the shade.

"I will now demonstrate the power of your juju," exclaims the Nigerian scornfully. He aims the dane-gun and, from a distance of perhaps several yards, blows away the chicken and a chunk of cement from the corner of the house. Little remains of the bird except a few feathers. "See!" he shouts righteously, waving his free arm at the dearly departed. "Juju doesn't work! Throw it away!"

Tanya will refuse to come to the North to teach. She does not want to be a modern woman in a conservative Muslim society where women are little more than chattel. I will understand that, will be quite willing to change posts after the wedding. It will give me a chance to experience another Nigeria—the coastal region of steaming jungles, slash-and-burn agriculture, Christian missions and animism, the traditional mixed in strange ways with Westernization.

I do not realize that this will be the first of many moves required by the perpetual dissatisfactions of Tanya. We will marry in an Ibo village, will conceive a son there, will see the violent birth of Biafra and the beginning of civil war. We will be ordered out of Nigeria on a half day's notice, will return to America in July of 1967.

We will teach in Vermont and California, will suffer culture shock as America attacks Vietnam and herself during the turn-on, tune-in, drop-out sixties. We will suffer guilt as two million Biafran children starve, as the nation dies at two and a half.

After graduate school, we will go overseas again, to teach in Micronesia and Turkey. In Micronesia Tanya will disagree violently with the administration of the school, will try to change it, will fail, will try to leave, but there will be no plane—no quick way to escape. She will begrudgingly remain through the year, fighting every day of every week for her idea of the way a Micronesian school ought to be run. In Turkey she will again grow angry with the school administration. She will leave for France to seek another degree while I remain in Izmir with our son.

When we return to America after five years abroad, I will find a college position in Michigan. She will also teach there for a while, will become dissatisfied, will fail at trying to redefine her job, will call the dean and president male chauvinists, will quit, will take a low-paying position at a private arts academy three hundred miles away. The next year she will go back to graduate school two states and eight hundred miles away, will live apart from me and her son for three years. Then she will find her own college teaching position a hundred miles away. By then she will have nearly four master's degrees and a Ph.D. In the summer she will do research in Canada, will want to return to France.

Again and again I will be told of my flaws—of how if I love her I will give up our home, friends, and work to follow her to wherever she wants to go—to the university, to Canada, to France. She will blame me for all of the imaginary flaws she sees in our son. She will blame me for every male who doesn't give her exactly what she demands and she will demand always that every job and every friendship and every community be redefined to her specifications.

In the end I will turn away from her and she will disappear into America's academia. She will move restlessly from university to university, from sabbaticals in Montreal or Paris to research in Dakar or Abidjan. Always her research will deal with the moral superiority of women. Always she will be driven, seeking always to drive herself and others as her mother once drove her. Eventually I will lose all contact with her, will no longer know where she lives or what she does. She will pass out of my life as if she had never existed.

She. Our son. I. Alone in America.

Somewhere to the south and far from any road, the only Stone Age people of Nigeria live atop hills that rise for hundreds of feet out of the flat plain. The hills are actually huge slabs of rock weathered into blocks that are tumbled together as if dropped from the arms of a mile-high giant child. Originally there was no soil at all. The hill people first climbed onto the hills in prehistory. Did they climb to escape slave raiders? Other enemies? No one knows. They carried sackfuls of soil from the plain, tucked the soil into flat crevices in the rock, carved cisterns, carried up building materials, planted.

Their rock protects them now as it has for a thousand years. Each mini-culture on each hill is unique. Each has its own language, its own religion, its own god. The hill folk know nothing of the turmoil on the plain—of the tribal hatreds and tribal politics; of looting and murder.

One day I will be sorry for everything. I will even be sorry I exist. I will think of suicide. I will learn about different kinds of handguns—prices, actions, pounds of impact, accuracy.

I will become apologetic for everything—for having literature to teach, for getting too many plush grants in too many plush places, for publishing stories and articles, for keeping my job.

She will say I am unfair, that the place will fold anyway, that I haven't stood up for her when others took advantage.

She will say I have lost my sense of adventure, that I am no different from all the other drones and spineless fools that make up America.

She will throw my title in my face as if it were something loathsome—"Professor! Professor! They actually call you that, and I've worked so hard and so long! What right do you have?"

She will hate me for getting up late, reading for hours, correcting student compositions too quickly.

I will apologize for sex. She will be a good lover but she will say, "I can't have you! Why can't I really have you?" She will tell me about the magic she once had with a pony-tailed recidivistic hippie folk dancer: "Just the touch of his hand was a bigger turn-on than I'll ever get from you. And I turned him down. He wanted sex, to fuck, and that's not me. If I had wanted that, I certainly wouldn't have married you!"

Words. An endless monologue interrupted only by "Well, don't you have anything to say?" My brain will freeze from the words. The words will drive me nuts—slamming their way through my skull, pounding against my chest, slapping my face. I will apologize for not throwing my life away and going with her to France. Always she will speak of France, as if it were the be-all and the end-all of everything. I will wish she had married some pale emaciated unathletic pseudo-Marxist lettuce-eating Parisian and had left me alone.

I will even apologize for disliking folk dancing but loving baseball. She will hate me for knowing Ted Williams's 1941 batting average. She will say it's a sign of my immaturity, of my inability to grow beyond little boys' games.

She will chase me with a knife and I will envision myself dead—boxed, looking good in a goddamned coffin with a Mary Kay smile on my frozen face and a Mormon suit and tie and, for the only time, a shiny pair of shoes.

She will blame me for our son's defection—"If you didn't stick us at the end of the earth, he'd visit more often"—and she will run away. Again and again.

Eventually I will turn to another woman, will have an affair with the shortstop of a barnstorming ladies' professional softball team. Tanya and I will go our separate ways. Alone. In America.

I go by taxi to the lorry park, a large open field on the edge of Maiduguri where lorries load passengers. Most of the lorries arrive already heavily loaded down with dozens of fifty-pound hemp sacks of peanuts, the local crop. On top of the peanuts they pile men, the occasional veiled woman, cardboard suitcases, wooden crates, bundles of clothes, pots and pans, sacks of produce, goats, chickens, sheep, dried fish from Lake Chad, and anyone or anything else that can find space to squeeze on. The trip to Kano

across the arid plain normally takes two days. The lorry I select is
going straight through to Lagos—a five-day trip. I sign on for
the whole distance at a cost of six pounds. My lorry is painted
bright orange and blue and is decorated everywhere with quota-
tions from the Koran and from oral tradition—GOD IS GREAT, AN
ELEPHANT IS A RABBIT IN ANOTHER TOWN, EAGLE EYES SEE
SMALL BACKS, EVIL WOMAN NO RIDE HERE.

I am assured by the driver that the lorry will leave at ten A.M.
the following morning. I arrive the next day by nine, throw my
pack high onto a peanut sack behind the cab roof, crouch on the
shady side of a nearby tree, and wait. The lorry park is stifling,
but there are food vendors in plywood stalls and soft-drink stands
with no walls but with roofs made of bundles of twigs supported
by posts. I consume several Coca-Colas and some quinine water.
Time creeps slowly past midday and the temperature rises. Even
the mosquitoes become too hot to fly. They settle in the shade and
stagger about as if drunk. As the hours pass, more and more
travelers arrive. By two the lorry is overflowing. Several travelers pay small sums to stand on the rear bumper.

By four the driver finally indicates we are about to leave, but
first I must pay two more pounds for the white man's privilege
of sitting in the cab itself with the driver and his assistant. I
prefer to ride on top with the others, but the driver is insistent.
He says he has already sold my space on top and I must come
inside. Reluctantly I agree and we are on our way. I climb into
the cab only to discover that we shall share the space with several
more peanut sacks and a goat. Somehow we find room and we
pull out.

The truck whines through the city's narrow streets in low
gear, groans noticeably as we pick up speed on the outskirts
of town, but then rides relatively smoothly once we are on the
open highway. The Kano road contains one center lane of tarmac.

We ride this until we meet another vehicle. Then we veer into the dirt lane and merge our clouds of dust as we pass. Fortunately traffic is rare and the tarmac is in good shape, with only the occasional pothole large enough to swallow a Japanese car.

Forty-two miles into the desert the lorry breaks an axle striking a pothole and we are stranded in a collection of mud and thatch compounds called Benisheik. The driver thumbs a ride on another lorry back to Maiduguri. I wait that evening for his return. I meet the local teacher and the headman, the *sarki*. We drink tea together and eat peppered chicken. The driver does not return. I sleep under the truck, using my pack as a pillow. The teacher apologizes for the inconvenience but hopes that I understand that I cannot be invited into any of their homes since it is forbidden—I might see their wives and daughters.

The driver finally returns with a new axle the following afternoon. He is apologetic but says it is not his fault. The lorry co-owner, a Lebanese, had already gone to the Lake Chad Club by the time the driver arrived in Maiduguri yesterday. By the time the owner left the club, he was very drunk and could not be spoken to until he had sobered up.

The day is spent in unloading the lorry, replacing the axle, and reloading. On the afternoon of the third day we are on our way again. The driver has slept very little for several days. He keeps awake by reciting from the Koran hour after hour, the lilting tones of Arabic filling up the cab above the whine of the gears.

We drive all night, all the next day, all the next night, and into the morning. Twice we stop in villages to eat and drink. The food is usually some kind of stew from a huge communal bowl set on rocks over a charcoal fire beside the road. The one spoon is passed from traveler to traveler unwashed. I skip the stew and buy bread, sardines, and a pepper chicken. I wash these down with quinine water, the bitter taste miraculously cutting my thirst.

On the final night before Kano we pass through a shower, the first rain I've seen in Nigeria. I climb onto the running board and stand there until the rain cloud falls behind. The air is cool, I am soaked, my legs are splashed with red mud to the tops of my thighs, and I am deliriously happy. The driver and his assistant eye me suspiciously, thinking I'm a bit mad.

We reach Kano with a broken shock. I am taken to the home of the co-owner of the lorry while more repairs are done. This owner is the brother of the man in Maiduguri. He has a palatial home with marble floors, imported European furniture, leather upholstery, a color TV, a tennis court, a pool, a large flower garden, and a guest room with a king-size bed. I stay there overnight and eat a magnificent breakfast of fresh tropical fruits, eggs, bacon, and toast before boarding the lorry for the trip south to the coast.

All day we travel uneventfully through the flat, featureless plain, the landscape gradually becoming less arid as we approach the border of the Western Region. Near Ilorin we add ourselves to the end of a long chain of stalled traffic. Two days earlier a lorry overturned across the highway on a bridge crossing a dry riverbed. No one can pass. Local people are getting rich selling food. Fortunately heavy equipment arrives from Ilorin the next day and shoves the lorry off the bridge into the riverbed.

The next day we reach the Yoruba city of Ibadan in Western Nigeria. I leave the lorry at the taxi park and join an overloaded bus traveling eastward to Benin. The bus travels on back roads, stopping in every little bush village to drop off and take on travelers, produce, animals, and crates. A journey of two hundred miles takes twenty-four hours. Still, I am lucky. Although I do not know it, another military coup has taken place in Lagos. Ironsi has been murdered, his body dumped into the bush where it will not be found for days. Ibo soldiers are being murdered in every barrack. On the main highways army barricades have been thrown up, and all traffic to the East has been stopped.

I reach Benin, sixty-eight miles from my destination, but it is evening and all traffic farther east has stopped. I am told that at night, bandits rule the roads—they rob and murder travelers. I pay a taxi driver an exorbitant sum to take me to Issele Uku, only eight miles from my destination. He agrees but drives very fast without lights. He insists he will run down anyone who appears in the road. Beside him on the seat he lays a machete which he often nervously fingers.

We reach Issele Uku without incident. There are four male Peace Corps Volunteers in the town. They all live together in the compound of Reverend Martin, a kind of theocratic dictator who runs the Baptist church, the Baptist high school, the Baptist teachers' college, and the Baptist hospital. Reverend Martin has his own generator and huge speakers in the trees of his compound. He plays hymns by Jim Reeves for hours every day. The hymns blast through the town, reminding all of its inhabitants that Reverend Martin is the boss.

I follow the hymns to the Volunteers, who have heard I was coming and are astounded that I got through. They tell me of the coup. All day Ibo refugees have been fleeing eastward in long convoys. The Volunteers feed me and give me a bed for the night. The next morning I am awakened at five by Jim Reeves. I breakfast, borrow a bicycle, and pedal along a bush road for the last eight miles.

It is the day before my wedding. I am happy. The morning is

cool compared to Maiduguri. The jungle is a rich tapestry of greens. I arrive at Tanya's home. She is inside drinking her third cup of coffee and trying to recover from a bottle of wine consumed after she heard of the coup. We embrace.

I begin the next twenty years of my life.

HEMINGWAY ON SEXUALITY

Hemingway had his first date when he was a junior in high school. He was not considered much of a lady's man until he returned from World War I in a tailored Italian officer's uniform that implied he'd been a soldier. Before that, the only women who usually surrounded him were his four sisters, his strong-willed mother, the cook, the nurse, and a couple of maids.

Hemingway had no qualms about saying that he knew all about sex as a teenager, that he had clap twice at an early age. He liked to say that he had visited a 258-pound Michigan whore who enjoyed him so much that she returned the two-dollar fee. On a trip to Sicily to visit a friend, he said he was kidnapped by the hostess of a hotel and kept as her gigolo for a week.

Later he said he had two Havana whores named Xenophobia and Leopoldina and that every woman he'd ever asked had said yes.

He liked to brag that he and Hadley had made love in Paris an average of one hundred times a month, that he had slept with Legs Diamond's girlfriend, that he had known Mata Hari.

BY THE EGGPLANTS

Through my window I watch the September wind pile brown leaves against the base of an adjacent building. Somewhere across the river that divides the campus the woman with whom I sleep is teaching biology to future nurses. Cheryl is an ideal teacher—always thoroughly prepared and always correct. She teaches biology because she's good at memorizing. Lists of muscles, of nerves, of organs, of parts of organs—she drills herself on them, makes them an integral part of herself.

"I've never comprehended people like you," she says, and she doesn't mean this to be a compliment. "You read a story and dig out all this stuff that I never see. Stuff you've put in there. I don't even see it after you've shown it to me."

And I want to tell her that I write stories, that I create words out of the ball of a pen, and that those words tell truths that all her lists of tissues and bones will never match. But I say nothing.

She enters her classroom at precisely ten o'clock and will lecture without interruption until the fifty allotted minutes have passed. Then she will return to her office to review meticulously the lecture she will give in her next class.

*   *   *

Today I am doing Hemingway. Ernest is one of my favorite writers and I get carried away with his words and with my own. We are reading "Indian Camp" and "The Doctor and the Doctor's Wife." The students ask freshman questions—unsophisticated and literal. Most of them are young women who resent having to read stories by a man they feel symbolizes male dominance, *machismo*, insensitivity to women. They ask me why I chose his short stories as a text. "Because Ernest loved Paris," I reply, "and so do I. And he loved Istanbul and Africa and so do I. He loved Michigan and disliked Chicago's suburbs. So do I." Their questions continue. Did Hemingway really watch his father perform a Caesarean with a jackknife and fishing line? Did his father really have a confrontation with an Indian named Dick Boulton? Why did the doctor's wife stay in that darkened room?

I point out the danger of reading biography into fiction. I begin the biography, detailing the events of Hemingway's early life that come out in the fiction. "Notice the transformation," I say. "The artist in the man transforms the personal into the myth, into the universal."

Most of the students are the same future nurses that Cheryl teaches. They want to know about Hemingway the man. "Tell us about his love life," says a scraggly-haired girl wearing faded sweatshirt and jeans. Earlier I had seen her park her battered pickup in the parking lot and had guessed the details of her life: early marriage; early motherhood; a husband who works hard and drinks harder; a yard decorated with snowmobiles, old tires, chain-saw parts. "Was Hemingway happy?" another girl asks.

"He killed himself," I say. The girls collectively suck in their breaths.

"Tell me about his wives," exclaims a voice in the back. "Did they love him?" I stare at the source of the voice, at the beautiful young woman in the blue sweater.

"I think they loved him," I say.

"Then there must have been a mistake," says the girl. "Men who are loved do not kill themselves."

"Sometimes love is not enough," I say.

The girl's green eyes flash mischievously and she bursts into a deep throaty laugh that startles in its vigor. "Is it enough for you?" she says and her mass of brown hair swirls about her face.

I don't know, I think to myself. "He had four wives," I say aloud. "One of his friends once accused him of taking every new woman in his life too seriously. 'The trouble with Ernest,' the friend said, 'is that he always thought that if he slept with her he had to marry her.' "

"And do you agree with that?" says the girl.

"I agree that Ernest seemed to believe that," I say.

"That's not what I'm asking," she says.

"I know," I say and again am swallowed up in that boisterous laugh. I stare into those French eyes and then pull myself away. We resume.

Cheryl is pretty but not beautiful. Her blonde hair falls to her waist. Her gray-blue eyes and marble complexion resent the sun.

She has spent her life doing whatever is correct. She studies hard, works hard, loves carefully.

Her day begins like this. She rises early and dresses herself in inner layers of white cotton and outer layers of wool as protection against the cold dawns. She does this winter and summer. In the kitchen in the gray light of sunrise she grinds fresh coffee beans from Zimbabwe and perks the coffee in the maker left clean and ready the night before on the sideboard. She eats a bowl of bran mixed with fresh fruit and raisins. She insists the bran keeps her normal. So does the coffee. She must have at least two cups if she is to avoid constipation. Just to be safe she has a third cup. Then a fourth.

As she eats and drinks she studies her biology text. She makes careful lists for her first lesson. Then she showers, makes up, dresses carefully in a business suit, brushes her hair. Before I stumble out of bed sometime after nine, she has departed for her first class, her briefcase packed tightly with ordered notebooks and the text. She does not trust herself behind the wheel on snowy days. If it is snowing, she walks the mile to her office. If it is clear, she drives her Volkswagen. In either case she arrives at her office with plenty of time to spare.

I go to my first class without breakfast, a cup of cafeteria coffee clutched in my hand. We're continuing with Hemingway. I try to remember what we covered yesterday. It doesn't matter. Each new lesson rises naturally out of each new story to be studied. The lesson is Hemingway's prose. Beautiful. Whole. Coherent. I sit down on top of the table in the front of the room. I notice without embarrassment that my jeans are worn white in the front and that the thread of one knee encircles a small hole. This morning my shirt, thank God, is not inside out. I pick up the bright green collected short stories of Hemingway and kiss it. The students burst out laughing.

"God, I love this stuff," I say. "Today we'll journey to Italy, to another time and place. Let's begin 'In Another Country.' "

*　　*　　*

I arrive home in the afternoon and turn up the thermostat until I sweat uncomfortably between my shoulder blades. Cheryl will be cold when she arrives. The kitchen table is covered with a disordered pile of my current reading. I collect the books—an odd collection about Tibet, Marco Polo, the Huron Mountains, baseball, Cicero, stained-glass windows—and carry them to my desk in the corner of the study. I balance the new pile on an old pile that already covers the desk top.

I decide to clean up a little so that Cheryl won't complain when she arrives. I vacuum the center of the living room and rehide the vacuum in the back of the hall closet. I check the toilet bowl for stains, find one, and rub it out with tissue. I flush the bowl clean.

I wash my hands and prepare supper. Tonight we'll have trout. Cheryl hates red meat and loves fish but hates the raw smell of it. I carry the fish outside while it is still wrapped tightly in layers of supermarket plastic. I unwrap it under a tree in the corner of the yard and spray it clean with the garden hose. I cut off the head and tail and carry these and the wrappings to the garbage can behind the house.

I return to the kitchen with the cleaned fish already wrapped tightly in tin foil and slide it on the broiler pan into the oven. After it is baked I will salt my portion separately. Cheryl is down on salt, says it's bad for the blood. She's also down on pepper, says it's too hot and kills the taste buds.

Cheryl soon arrives. She's cold. Her feet are swollen. She unwraps and stretches out on the couch, her feet up. While I busy myself in the kitchen, she tells me about her students, about her lesson.

I say *Oh*. And *Ah*. And *Mmhm*.

I think always of those green eyes, the tremendous life in that laugh.

*   *   *

On the third day of Hemingway she stops me in the hall. "I've got to leave your class," she says. I've learned her name—Candy.

"Why?" I ask. "You're doing very well."

"That's not it," she says, shaking her brown locks out of her eyes.

"You have French eyes," I say. "Depthless. Green. Full of life."

"Don't say that," she says. Her hand flicks out and grazes my chest, then snaps back as if burned. "I'm falling in love with you."

"How do you know?" I ask. I want to touch her, to hold her, to possess her. I do nothing.

Cheryl stretches on the living room couch and waits for supper. Her radio plays Stravinsky as she reads the latest issue of *Ms*. She has wrapped herself in two afghans but complains to me, forty feet away in the kitchen, that her knees and feet are cold. "The new math instructor has terrible body odor," she informs me. "I could still smell her after she vacated my office. She came in to say hello. That nervous odor. You know what I mean?"

"Yeah," I say. My radio plays the evening news. I bring her a glass of South African wine. She likes the idea of its origin, says it's exotic. "But politically unpalatable," I say. "What do you mean?" she asks. I return to the kitchen, to my beer and book. The wine will settle her nervous stomach. She says she needs it to digest my cooking.

I stir the chili as it bubbles on the stove. "There'll be a ballgame on TV tonight," I shout.

"How can you watch that stuff?" she asks. "It's so violent. I'll have to study upstairs."

"It's not football," I say.

"I thought baseball season was over weeks ago," she replies.

"There's a little less than a month to go," I answer. "This is the pennant drive now."

"I hope we're not having beans," she says. "My stomach's already gassy. Did you dust this week? I hate to bring it up again, but it's your job and you keep putting if off. And come out here. I hate to have to shout into the kitchen."

"I can hear you fine," I say as I come to the doorway between the rooms. "I cleaned up a little when I got home."

"You didn't dust," she says. "And your desk's a mess."

"I could make you really happy," Candy says as I approach. I'm hurrying to class because I'm already late. She's been waiting in the hall.

"I'm already with someone else," I say, trying not to stare at the curve of her hips, the cleavage visible above the low neckline of her red blouse.

"I could make you happier," she says. "I need you and love you."

After class she waits for the others to leave. We linger by the blackboard. I want to fall into her eyes, to bury myself in her full lips.

"You're Hemingway," she says. "When you read him, you become him. I read your stories. They have them in the library. You write like him—not as well, of course, but okay." That laugh bursts from her, ricocheting off the walls. "I was in love for seven years but he left me. I go by our house sometimes but he's in there with someone else. If I catch her alone, I'll tear out her eyes."

"Why me?" I ask.

"I don't know," she says. "It just happens."

She lives with her mother, who would not approve. Her mother considers her a slut. "Just because I've had lots of dates," Candy says. Her mother's Catholic.

"Where can I see you?" I ask.

"At work. I shelve at the IGA. Meet me by the eggplants tomorrow afternoon. I work every night until ten. Except Friday. Fridays are for fun."

"The eggplants," I repeat.

She laughs happily, that deep-seated laugh of pure joy. "Or the breakfast cereals," she says. "Linger with me over the Frosted Flakes."

"You're kidding."

"I wish I were. I have to work. My dad left us years ago. He's an alcoholic, working construction somewhere out West—maybe in Arizona. I've been on my own since I was sixteen."

"But you're still living at home," I say.

"That's a recent thing," she explains. "I left home at sixteen but now I'm back. My mother leaves the door unlocked and I come in and sleep on the couch. I pay all my own expenses—car, clothes, food. My mother doesn't have much, and there are lots of kids."

I walk with her to the parking lot. Her car is a wreck—a green Corvette with a bashed hood, a broken light, a crumpled fender. "Three accidents in the last month." She grins and introduces me to the car. "This is David. I drive him too fast."

*   *   *

"My mother is coming next week," says Cheryl. She is adding ammonia and Top Job to the wash bucket. "This place has to be absolutely clean. Everything. Not just your usual superficial cleaning. Windows. Woodwork. Everything."

"Which day is she coming?" I open a beer and flip the top across the kitchen in the general vicinity of the open plastic wastebasket.

"Saturday. She's flying into Green Bay. I don't want her taking the local airline. Not with their record. She wouldn't like it. She's used to the best. First class only."

"That's two hundred miles!" I show my disgust by swigging noisily at the beer. "I'm not driving four hundred miles just to pick up your mother!"

"You'll be on her good side then," she says. "She already disapproves."

"What do you mean? What have I ever done to her?"

"We're not married." Cheryl says this as if she agrees with her mother—as if she too considers me some kind of pervert for not marrying her. "She wants to spend time with you. I told her you're wonderful, but she wants us to marry."

I guzzle down the remainder of the beer, knowing it will irritate her. "I'll pick up your mother if I can make the trip enjoyable. I'll ask Paavo if he wants to go to Milwaukee to a ballgame. We'll pick up your mother on the way back."

"You expect me to stay here and clean while you play? Just like a man! You're all the same!" Cheryl drives her cleaning rag viciously into the pail of suds, splashing gray water and soap onto the floor.

"If you want your mother, that's how it'll have to be."

"You forget that she's a doctor's wife." Cheryl gets down on her knees and begins to clean the kitchen floor, her arm extended as she pushes the wash rag in larger and larger circles. She is wearing a babushka, a remnant of her Croatian ancestry. I add my empty beer bottle to the bags of empty bottles in the back hallway. I go to the fridge to get another beer. "My mother's used to the best," says Cheryl. "You'll have to drive carefully. She's used to a clean car and clean restaurants. None of your usual places. She especially likes those large shrimp from Mexico, the fresh ones. Maybe you could find a place that serves them."

"Are you kidding? The only seafood you'll find on a menu from the restaurants in those little Wisconsin towns is frozen fish sticks and fries."

"You could at least try to find a seafood place. My mother's a very sensitive woman."

"Does she stay in a darkened room?" I ask, recalling Hemingway's "The Doctor and the Doctor's Wife."

"What? I don't understand. Sometimes you're so indecipherable."

Candy and I have a tryst in the aisle by the rutabagas. I'm nervous and seek an excuse for coming. "I just came to say you're beautiful, but I feel ridiculous, standing here by the rutabagas," I say.

"Buy something," she says. "It'll make you feel better. Here. Get some of these." She shoves a bag of carrots into my hand. Her lips mouth "I love you" as I retreat.

Paavo is my best friend, a backwoods Finn who grew up here in Michigan's Upper Peninsula where we both teach. Paavo is my only real friend—the kind of guy who would help me out of any tight spot that didn't lead directly to prison. He and I share a lot, but we're also very different. I've had a full-time job at the university in Coppertown for years, but Paavo just teaches a class or two, earning just enough money for survival. Sometimes he takes a term off altogether. He gets away with it because the department chair has a crush on him. I can see it in her eyes and hear it in her voice whenever he speaks to her. She always blinks in a funny way, and her voice shakes. A year ago a rumor circulated that Paavo was having an affair with her, but I can't believe that was true since Paavo has exquisite taste in women. The university has unspoken rules against fraternization between faculty and students, but Paavo has dated all sorts of students. He's a free spirit who ignores most rules and always tries to maximize his free time.

Paavo says he needs lots of free time to experience life, to read, and to write. While I spend hours preparing lessons and correcting compositions, Paavo comes and goes. He skis a lot, fishes, and generally enjoys life. He loves to eat. He fixes his own gourmet masterpieces inspired by India, China, or some other exotic place. Sometimes he passes on his recipes, but I only occasionally try them since Cheryl hates spicy food.

Our school year ends in early May. Paavo and I usually plan a fishing trip on the Sturgeon River for the first week of vacation. Then we make Paavo's winter wood on forty acres he owns out at the end of the Keweenaw Peninsula along Lake Superior. Paavo uses a lot of wood during the cold months. He lives in an abandoned one-room schoolhouse at the end of a dirt road about seven miles north of Coppertown. Because he's never fully insulated the place, he must keep a fire going all winter.

I've come to Paavo because I don't know what to do about Cheryl and the girl in the supermarket. I value his advice because he's the sort of guy who drives women crazy. This comes from his habit of dating two or three women more or less at the same time. Every so often one of them begins to take him seriously or actually falls in love. Then she gets possessive, insists that Paavo make a choice. So far he's always chosen to say good-bye.

We sit around Paavo's potbellied stove, drink beer, and chew on smoked salmon. "Come on, buddy, own up," he says. "You've been holding out on me."

"Cheryl wants me to marry her," I explain. "A guy can't be fancy-free forever. Eventually we all have to take responsibilities."

"Bullshit!" Paavo reaches for more fish from the plate on the floor between our chairs. "Who's been giving you that line? Not Cheryl I hope. It sounds like her. I don't want to piss you off, but she can be an aggressive little bitch. She's always finding fault. You don't love her, do you?"

"Hell no!"

"Then how can you be serious about this marriage bullshit?" Paavo gives me one of his patented boy-are-you-a-dumb-shit looks. "I want to give you some serious advice, Buddy. This is straight from the heart. No baloney. One of these days some reasonably pretty woman will realize the advantages in attaching herself to you. She'll look right behind that ugly face of yours and see the size of your bank account. Then she'll fall all over you."

"And I won't see through that?" I ask.

"Not if she's cute. You have no experience. An amazing number of women are predatory, especially these so-called progressive ones—the liberated types. They take everything. They want you to be sexy like a traditional male is supposed to be and yet they'll grab you right by the nuts if you try to be like that. It's a no-win situation."

"You ought to know." I mildly resent Paavo's comment on my lack of experience.

"Hell, I don't know what I'm talking about," laughs Paavo loudly as he chews on more fish and wipes the oil off his fingers onto his pants. "I don't even have a bank account. I'll bet Cheryl has told you the advantages of marriage a hundred times. At the same time I'll bet she's called it some kind of slavery for the woman—a selling of her soul to the patriarchal system."

"No, she hasn't, but she's really pushing for it. Her mother's coming next Saturday. I'm supposed to pick her up in Green Bay. You want to come along? We can catch a Brewers game."

Paavo agrees. I tell him about my student who works in the supermarket.

"She want to marry you too?" Paavo asks.

"I think so."

"Tell me what you like about Cheryl."

"Nothing." I really can't think of anything even though I want to come up with something. Otherwise, why do I live with her?

"And the student?"

'She excites me. Her body. Eyes, hair, breasts, legs, everything."

"No reason to marry," Paavo says. "Everybody's got a body. What do you know about her?"

"Not much."

"Stay single. Get to know the student. Be honest with Cheryl. Tell her to get lost if that's what you really want."

"I'm not sure," I say.

"You're one confused guy!" exclaims Paavo.

In the middle of the game Cheryl shouts from the top of the stairs. I get up, turn down the volume, go to the stairwell, and ask what she wants. "Could you bring me some tea?" she asks. "My feet are cold."

"Jesus Christ!" I say almost loud enough for her to hear as I tramp into the kitchen. Every damned night she needs tea for her cold feet.

"What?" she says.

"Sure," I shout. "Any particular kind?"

"Herbal," she shouts back. "And tomorrow, if you have time, could you do a load of towels? I'm almost out of washcloths."

"I just did them the other day," I shout as I prepare the tea with hot water from the kettle on the back of the stove. How can she drink this herbal shit? I ask myself for the thousandth time. Even the smell of it makes me want to gag.

"I go through washcloths fast," she shouts. "Unlike some people around here, I keep myself clean by washing thoroughly several times a day."

"There's so much power coursing through you when you're in class," she says. "So much energy. And excitement. You make me feel happy just listening to you. Your voice soothes me, makes me forget my own cares. I don't give a damn about Hemingway and his stories, but I love *your* Hemingway and *your* interpretations of his stuff. Hemingway gets transformed by you. He becomes you. I want to go to Paris and Madrid and Italy and all those other places Hemingway wrote about, but I want to go with *you*.

"You would respect me. The men around here don't respect women, but you do. I can tell that from everything you say.

"I also could make you happy. Maybe you don't believe that. I like sex. It's the most wonderful thing in the world. I could make you very happy that way. And I'm basically a happy person."

A stream riffles over rocks. We are in a park full of flowers. It seems to be perfumed with flowers—violets and roses and

Queen Anne's lace. Yet there is really only grass, a great expanse of green surrounding picnic tables. In the distance several young couples watch their young children run.

"Will you go to a motel with me?" I ask.

"I'm afraid," Candy replies.

"Afraid of me?" I squeeze her hand.

"Of losing you. I'm afraid that if we make love you'll run away from me, retreat back to Cheryl, cut me off from your life."

"Why do you think such a thing?"

She looks away vacantly, staring into a distance I cannot see. She says nothing.

"Maybe we'd better go back," I say, disappointment clear in my voice.

"You'll never know how much I love you," she says, still looking away. "While you linger between Cheryl and me, aren't you afraid of losing me forever? Aren't you worried that some young man my own age will come along and sweep me off my feet?"

"Yes," I say and squeeze her hand.

"There's no one out there," she says. "No one at all. You're all I want, but I'm afraid of you."

I sit shirtless in the relative coolness of my kitchen. Indian summer for one day has brought the temperatures into the eighties. All of me—heart, body, mind, soul—thinks of her, yearns for her. This morning at the IGA, under the phony red and yellow tent set up over the produce section to give the illusion of a harvest fair, I wanted to take her. Some old folks were buying turnips and squash. A breeze through the open back door of the kitchen is perfumed with her, with an intangible but real touch of her. Her name is magic. I recite it. Candy . . . Candy . . . Candy. The name fills me with the purest of pleasure.

* * *

Somewhere on a hill a half mile away, she shelves Fruit Loops and granola, moves among her apples, oranges, and bananas. I sit here alone as if I were with her, inside her, a part of her, and yet it's as if she were a thousand miles away, irretrievably lost to me by time and space. I suffer an agony so acute that I want to die. How did I end up in this dilemma? How did I come to live with someone like Cheryl? I think we met at a faculty picnic, but I'm not sure. Cheryl says I knocked her down during an interfaculty soccer match. That's her version, not mine. I'm not sure when she took over my life. I've never been sure with women. Before Cheryl I dated only the uglier faculty women and occasionally picked up some basket case in a bar. I wish I was more like Hemingway. When he was a young man he went for older, more experienced women. His first love, Agnes Von Kurowsky, was seven years older, his first wife eight. As he grew older he went after the excitement and beauty of younger women like the Italian teenager who became Renata in *Across the River and Into the Trees*.

"There's an epidemic of venereal disease among the students," says Cheryl. She is sitting wrapped in an afghan at the kitchen table, drinking herbal tea and reading about livers. Her feet are wrapped in a double layer of winter stockings.

"How do you know?" I'm stuffing artichokes with a mixture of ground turkey, onion, raisins, capers, and catsup. I decide to wash some baking potatoes.

"Oh, it's all over campus," Cheryl answers. "Everyone's talking about it. I believe in women's liberation, but today's young women take it too far. They'll sleep with anybody and give them all gonorrhea, syphilis, AIDS, and whatever. They don't seem to care. They don't know the meaning of love. It's understandable, of course. Most are from divorced families, have complexes about their fathers, and have been sleeping around since they turned fifteen."

"Do you want one potato or two?"

"You know I never eat more than one." She looks up from her chapter on livers and checks out my reaction. "Do they ever flirt with you?"

"I'll bake you one medium-sized one," I say, scrubbing away at potato skin in the sink.

"I know they do," she says. "Just stay away from them. I don't want to have to drag both of us to a clinic just because you wanted a few moments of fun."

"There's a good movie downtown tonight." I lay the potatoes in the oven and set the temperature. Everything's ready. I just have to wait for it to get done.

"Is it American?" Cheryl's asked this before but I ignore the stupidity of the question.

"Of course it's American. What in hell other kind of movie would they have at a local theater?" I recall the last foreign film that played in Coppertown—*Mad Max Beyond Thunderdome*. That was years ago.

"You don't have to get angry and swear," she says. "They're always so violent. What is it?"

"*The Killing Fields.*"

"Even the title is ugly." She goes back to her foul-smelling tea and her description of livers. "No. You go. Maybe Paavo or someone else will go with you."

"Maybe."

"I hate that stuff. It doesn't have Robert Redford in it, does it?"

"It's about Cambodia." I know she doesn't even know what that is.

"I don't even want to think about it," she says.

*　*　*

I wear a black Greek fisherman's hat to class. It matches the
Maine sea-captain's coat that I inherited from my grandfather. I
have no idea where he got it since he worked in a New England
textile factory all his life. Candy says she loves the hat and coat.
"They make you very handsome," she says. "They make me
proud to be near you. Plus the coat shows off your chest. I love
your chest. I want it to be mine."

And what is this infatuation of ours based upon? Is it as
ethereal as air, as false as cotton candy? I am baffled.

"You should marry a doctor or someone else with money." I sit
in the rocker correcting compositions, scratching red lines through
misspellings, incorrect apostrophes, misplaced commas. "Not
some nickel-and-dime schoolteacher and would-be author."

"Don't run yourself down," says Cheryl. She is curled up on
the couch, the afghan over her shoulders. Her briefcase is open
beside her and she is doing lab reports.

"It's true," I say.

"Those are my mother's values, not mine. You're good to
me." She looks up from a pile of papers and smiles. She doesn't
do that very often. "You cook wonderful meals. Of course I
often get stomachaches from the spices, but that's not entirely
your fault. And you clean the house. I usually have to do it over
again, but you try. And you're good to me in lots of other ways.
I don't think I could be happy without you. Plus you help me
grow. You know so much. Even if most of it is pretty silly. And
you put up with my eccentricities. Where else could I find
someone as good as you?"

"I'm a bastard," I say but don't explain. I'm thinking of
Candy in the supermarket.

"My feet are cold," she says. "Will you rub my feet? Please?"

"Yeah," I say but sound reluctant.

"It's okay. Go to Milwaukee to the game. I want you to have fun."

I put down my papers, lean forward, and take her foot between my hands. I rub.

On the way back from Green Bay the doctor's wife never stops talking. She sits broad-assed in the backseat and practically shouts the intimate trivia of her life. Paavo and I learn all about her constipation, her inability to sleep at night, the backaches she gets from traveling. She tells us about her two-week stay in a California fat farm—about the diet, the exercises, the staff. She spends a half hour raving about some lady that she played golf with the other day. "She told me right to my face, 'Why, Vanessa, you ought to hear all the things the women in this town say about you.' I couldn't believe she said that right to my face. I think it's probably because she's jealous of our new home at the country club. I mean, it is the best home in the town. She considers herself religious too—a real goody-goody. I hate people like that!" The doctor's wife goes on to tell us all the details of her new home—the furnishings, the number of rooms, the color of the wallpaper, the cost of modern high-tech plumbing, the myriad accessories necessary for the backyard pool, the amount of water used in the garden, the cost of Mexican help as opposed to black help.

When we leave Wisconsin's farmlands behind and enter Michigan's forests, she complains of claustrophobia. She prefers Arizona's open spaces and its "cute little deer paths." We stop at what locals would consider an expensive, high-class restaurant. The doctor's wife finds nothing on the menu worth eating. She discards the menu and asks the waitress if they have this or that. She goes through a long list of exotica. They don't have any of it. She gives up and orders only tea. They don't have that either. This is coffee country. Paavo and I eat fried chicken with mashed potatoes out of a box and green beans floating in water.

The doctor's wife, Paavo, and I arrive in Coppertown. I stop at the IGA, ostensibly to pick up some groceries. Candy is piling lettuce into a soft green pyramid in the middle of the greengrocer shelves. Her eyes light up when she sees me. "I'm walking on air," she says, a ball of iceberg in each hand. "You make me feel that way."

"I'm glad." I feel hot, dirty, and tired after the five-hour drive. "I want to marry you."

"Are you sure?" Her eyes are gleaming.

"I want to marry you," I say again. The words taste like truffles on my lips. "We may have to find an apartment. At least for now. It might get messy. I don't know. I only know how I feel."

"I love you too," she coos, and that wonderful laugh billows out of her, rolls in happy waves down the aisle. Suddenly her eyes grow dark and piercing. She stiffens.

A younger man with tight curls and a wisp of beard steps past me from behind. He plants a full kiss on her lips, holds it, steps back, places his hands on her shoulders, and smiles. "I'll pick you up at ten," he says and then is gone.

"Who was that?" I'm not sure what to say or do. I'm terribly confused.

"My boyfriend."

"Your boyfriend."

"Yes." Candy begins to pile more lettuces as if nothing important had happened.

"I didn't suspect. You said you live with your mother."

"Don't worry." It's obvious she wants to reassure me. "I only stay with him sometimes. I don't love him. I love you—only you. I want to marry you—to have your baby. Only one. But I do want one. I even have a name already picked out. It'll be a boy and I'll name it Nick."

"How can you stay with him if you don't love him? How can he stay with you?"

"And how can you stay with Cheryl when you detest her?"

I realize the double standard of my question. "Touché!" I say. "I'm sorry. I shouldn't have said that."

"Anyway, I lie to him. I tell him I love him, but I don't. If I can have you, I'll tell him the truth. Until then, you don't expect me to wait for these moments in the store, do you? I need someone. I'm a one-guy-at-a-time girl, but I do need someone. Always. I need you. I want to be with you."

"Always?" It's as if I suddenly need the security of her answer. "Forever?"

"Forever is a long time," she replies.

Paavo has entered the store. He sizes up the situation immediately and hurries to my side. I introduce him to Candy, tell her he's my best friend. "We're getting married," I add.

"Hey, that's great!" Paavo slaps me on the back and gives Candy a big hug. "Congratulations. So, Buddy, you finally made the big leap, the big decision. She's beautiful. It looks like I'll have to find a new fishing partner and a new woodcutter."

"That won't happen," I assure him. Candy looks very happy, and I feel wonderful for the first time in a long time—the kind of wonderful that penetrates to the soul, that gives meaning to life, that lasts a lifetime.

"If you two need a place to stay, you can move in with me," says Paavo. "It'll have to be temporary. No more than three months."

"That's great," I say.

"I have to go shelve Hi Ho crackers," says Candy. "After that I'll be in the pickles. I'll shelve my boyfriend too."

"Let's get out of here, Buddy," urges Paavo. "Your ex–possible future mother-in-law is getting anxious. The doctor's wife. Remember?" I had almost forgotten. Paavo grabs my arm and pushes me down the aisle. "You can spare him for a little while, Candy. He'll be back later. I'm happy to have met you. Hey, I never heard of anybody finding a wife by the lettuce." Candy waves as we depart and heads for the cracker aisle.

We go out the door. The doctor's wife—a carbon copy of Cheryl in too many ways—sits erect and patient in the backseat. Her heavy Navajo jewelry—necklace, earrings, bracelets, rings—glistens like brimstone. In a moment I will drive her to her daughter. They will embrace and talk rapidly. At some point they will argue. They always argue. They're so much alike that they can agree on nothing.

I will pack a few things, will tell Cheryl I'm leaving. If she asks, I'll tell her about Candy, about the eggplants.

We get in the car.

HEMINGWAY AND COMPETITION

Sherwood Anderson, an important Chicago writer immediately after World War I, met young Hemingway, liked him, and when he learned that Ernest and Hadley were going to Italy as newlyweds, urged the couple to choose Paris instead. Ernest took Anderson's advice, in part because Anderson gave Ernest letters of introduction to a number of important literary figures of Paris, such as Ezra Pound and Gertrude Stein. Anderson later urged his own publisher to accept Ernest's first full-size book, *In Our Time*. In return for such help, Ernest viciously satirized Anderson in *The Torrents of Spring*.

Gertrude Stein helped Ernest with his prose and introduced him to a number of important writers and artists in Paris. Ernest later described her as a coarse, loud-mouthed, jealous, and malicious woman.

Early in Ernest's career, before he had written much, Ford Madox Ford made him an assistant editor of the *Transatlantic Review* and offered advice that furthered Ernest's career. In return Ernest made fun of Ford in *A Moveable Feast*.

F. Scott Fitzgerald helped Ernest get his second publisher,

Scribner's—Fitzgerald's own. Fitzgerald also read the manuscripts of *The Sun Also Rises* and *A Farewell to Arms* and helped to make important changes in each. Ernest ridiculed Fitzgerald in "The Snows of Kilimanjaro" and in *A Moveable Feast*.

THE GAME

Jeff and Susan were living in the eighties but trying to be flower children of the sixties by driving endlessly across the continent like Jack Kerouac and Neal Cassady of the forties and fifties.

They had met at Berkeley twenty years earlier, in 1969, during the heyday of the subculture, when Berkeley was a Mecca for hippies from all over the world. Jeff had come to Berkeley from a working-class family in Chicago. He had hitched across the country in five days, catching one long ride in a truck and an assortment of shorter lifts in cars. He was a high school dropout with a dream of playing drums in a rock band. Back then Jeff had a pony tail and drug-haunted eyes. For a whole year after his arrival he wore the same unwashed jeans, a leather vest, and lots of beads.

Jeff and Susan wandered aimlessly up and down Telegraph Avenue, pausing to greet friends, smoke a little weed, shoot a little dope, and talk endlessly about the pig culture and the pop scene. Sometimes they whiled away entire days on the beach, drinking cheap wine and reading about bohemians of the past— the Beats, the Greenwich Village crowd, the expatriates in Paris in the twenties. Susan's background was very different from

Jeff's. Her family was wealthy and she was a pre-law student at the university. She wore clean granny dresses, very expensive jewelry that called attention to itself, and suede boots that she had purchased for five hundred dollars on a shopping spree during a summer trip to Montreal. Susan played at being hip but had other options. Jeff had no options.

In 1970 Susan and Jeff drifted apart. He became more deeply involved in the drug culture and moved to the Haight District in San Francisco. Susan met an already successful lawyer at a party given by one of her father's friends. She married him three months later.

Years passed. Susan lived in a $200,000 home in the eucalyptus-lined hills above the campus. Every year she drove another new economy car—not because it was inexpensive but because it was convenient for parking. Sometimes the cars were blue, sometimes red or beige. Her husband drove black Lincolns.

They had a daughter. Susan dressed her in frilly dresses. Whenever the daughter cried, Susan handed her to the nurse, a dark-haired short woman from El Salvador. An assortment of cooks cooked and maids cleaned.

In the meantime Jeff lingered with the subculture as it died a slow death. He drifted from San Francisco to a commune in New Mexico. He held an assortment of unsatisfying odd jobs at gas stations, on construction crews, in video stores. He moved to the Gulf Coast and worked on an oil rig. He wandered north, working on ranches and in lumber camps. All of his life was a series of dead ends. Finally he drifted back to Berkeley in 1985, desperately seeking the youthful dreams that had brought him there in 1969.

Susan met him by chance in a shopping mall. She was recently divorced and desperately unhappy. Her husband had left her for another, younger woman. Her daughter had died in a freak accident. The girl had tripped while running with garden shears in her hand, had fallen forward and driven the point of the shears into her throat. She had bled to death in minutes, Susan holding her convulsing body and screaming.

Using the considerable sum from Susan's settlement, she and Jeff had gone on the road, both seeking the failed dreams that they hoped lay somewhere just beyond the constantly receding horizon.

Many thousands of miles later, in midsummer of 1989, blasts of hot air from open windows failed to cool Susan or Jeff as their dusty Volkswagen approached an undistinguished village in central Illinois. Susan drove with her left hand. With her right she tried to cool off by opening the top buttons of her blouse. Occasionally Susan glanced toward Jeff, slouched against the passenger door. Today Jeff had been intransigent, mutely twisting into uncomfortable positions and nervously puffing cigarettes until hot ash threatened his lips.

Susan directed the rattling car carefully past nondescript buildings of a tiny shopping area. Then she swung sharply left to enter a residential street which led abruptly into flat prairie.

"Hey, where are you taking us?" Jeff asked as rough potholes jerked him to attention. "I thought we were heading further south until tonight. A delay on some dirt road will foul up our schedule."

"What schedule?" Susan laughed at the ludicrousness of the idea. "We haven't had a schedule in years. What's with you lately? Why are you so damned jumpy? Lately you've had to get as many miles as possible out of this old wreck. All those miles— it's almost as if you were pushing yourself instead of this ancient car." Susan lost control—her voice now hard and angry. "Jeff, for years we've been frantically crossing and recrossing this damned country. What difference does it make how fast we do it? Who cares? Are you trying to get in a record book or something?"

Jeff no longer listened. Instead he searched the roadside for familiar signs. There were none. Flat, dull landscape blended into hundreds of others Susan and he had seen.

"Pay attention to me!" Susan snapped. Jeff tilted his head to send a cursory look of disdain toward Susan before he again gazed outward across the monotonous flat land. "We don't need to be pushing on," Susan continued. "There's nothing further south that we haven't already seen. We can pitch a tent out here somewhere instead of closer to Cairo." After pausing, she added, "Anyway, we've been out here before."

Jeff squinted hard at the scorched, sparsely wooded country. He could discern no unique, memory-laden quality in stands of trees or open fields of wilted cornstalks. "When were we here?" he asked.

"A long time ago," Susan said. Jeff waited expectantly, but she added nothing. She leaned toward her side window, her face catching the stream of warm air that tossed long brown hair about her shoulders.

"All places look the same," whined Jeff as he fidgeted. Dust and heat choked his lungs and soaked his shirt with gritty sweat.

"Of course you don't remember," said Susan. Her eyes briefly rose to Jeff's sunburned face. She smiled wispily before she again concentrated on driving.

Minutes later Susan turned onto a single-lane dirt track that led across a weed-infested field toward a stand of cottonwood trees atop a slight rise. "Listen, Jeff," she said. "I think I can remember a tiny lake about a mile beyond these trees. We camped beside it one night a long time ago. There's a lovely little beach."

"You and your beaches!" snorted Jeff as he slouched deeper in the seat and thrust bare feet onto the diminutive dash. "I'll bet you've got a map in your head of every damned beach in America."

"Why do you suddenly dislike beaches so much?" Susan asked playfully. "You used to like them a lot. Now you say you don't. You're being contradictory. Sometimes you're a real pain in the ass that way." She reached over and rubbed her hand against his shoulder, trying to lighten his mood. In the last few months he had often been moody—bubbling over with enthusiasm one minute and lost inside himself the next.

"I can't stand beaches!" growled Jeff, sitting upright and pulling away from her touch. He rubbed streams of sweat out of his hair. "They're so damned hot. The sand gets between my toes and leaves red itchy marks."

"You're such a spoilsport sometimes," said Susan. "There are shade trees just behind the beach. You can sit there and cool off while I get a bit of sun."

"The ground will be damp near the water," argued Jeff. "There are probably flies—millions of stingers."

"No flies," replied Susan. "It hasn't rained around here for days. Everything's getting brown."

"Have it your way," said Jeff, his face smoldering. His words sounded innocent enough but Susan knew what they meant. If he disliked the beach, he'd get back at her later. He'd probably do it by giving her the silent treatment. That had been his method lately. She wondered how much longer she'd be able to put up with his moods.

At the lake they passed a private property sign nailed to a tree. The car followed a dirt track along the shore for a short distance.

When they reached the beach, Susan parked under a poplar. They stepped onto the wet, lumpy sand. Apparently no one had visited the tiny, secluded spot recently. Susan was elated. "Imagine finding a lake with no one on it!" she exclaimed.

"I wouldn't exactly call it a lake," said Jeff. "It looks more like an oversized farm pond. I suppose you noticed the sign. We'll probably have an irate farmer after us with a shotgun."

"Oh, no one takes those signs seriously," chided Susan. "It's probably posted to keep out hunters. Farmers have to protect stock."

"Maybe," conceded Jeff, "but if we end up in jail, remember who drove us here."

Susan ignored his childish threat. After a tentative survey, she chose a sunbathing spot near the water's edge. She slipped quickly out of her clothes and hung her sweaty blouse and jeans to dry on tree branches. Then she snuggled down on the sand.

Jeff was dizzy with the heat. His back itched infuriatingly from constant rubbing against the car seat. Still irritated that he and Susan were not moving south, he cursed the sun and fled toward a nearby poplar. He lined himself up in the narrow shade of the trunk, adjusted his back against the base, and pretended to sleep.

After a while Susan asked, "Aren't you going to swim? The water will cool you off."

Jeff ignored the query. "We should be moving," he said. "I'm getting nervous just sitting here. Time's passing."

"Let it pass," said Susan. "Come over here by me so I don't have to shout."

"You're not shouting," answered Jeff. "You're just speaking loudly. Anyway, it's too hot near the water. I'm going to stay right here in the shade."

"Why do you have to be such a spoilsport?" Susan cried as she rolled over onto her stomach and felt the warm touch of the sun on her buttocks.

"I'm not," Jeff replied.

Silent minutes passed until Susan lifted her head from the beach to face Jeff. "Hey, I've got an idea," she said expectantly. "Why don't we play another game?"

"What kind of game this time?" Jeff asked, his voice heavy. The rotator cuff in his left shoulder was aching again—an old injury from lumberjacking days—and he felt old, as if his joints were about to crumble in the heat.

"I don't know," Susan replied. "I'm sure we can think of something. Maybe we can start with where you'd like to be right now. Choose some place. It could be anywhere in the world."

"It's hot," Jeff replied. "I'd like to be somewhere cool. The trouble is that we've played this damned game too many times. I can't think."

"Try!" urged Susan as she entered enthusiastically into the fantasy. "Think of a place that's cool. Think hard."

"Paris," said Jeff abruptly. "Long gray days, with a fine rain falling. It's the 1920s."

"How did you get there?" Susan asked as she rubbed her stomach softly against clutching sand. She thought of *A Moveable Feast*, of how she and Jeff had spent a whole summer day on a beach south of San Francisco reading that book together. They had planned to go to Paris then. Why hadn't they?

Jeff concentrated on another life. "I'm a man of the world, a writer. Like Hemingway. I work when I feel like it but get rich anyway. I have a loft for writing in the mornings and drink with my bar buddies in the evening. Scott Fitzgerald and I get drunk together. We pick up street whores. In Paris most of the street whores are beautiful."

Susan stretched out in the heat like a cat lazy from hunting. "Tell me about the whores of Paris," she said.

"The cheapest ones are stringy and mathematical," Jeff said, his voice gathering excitement as he entered into his role. "In the Bois de Boulogne the low-class whores rush the act of love to a nervous completion. Girls stand in pairs or alone along the road during rush hour to or from middle-class suburbs. When traffic stalls at red lights, girls urge frustrated commuters out of cars. Behind nearby bushes they perform one-minute tricks for twelve francs."

"One minute? My God!" laughed Susan as she thrust bare buttocks into the air and dug toes into the sand.

"You won't believe what happens to me one day," said Jeff. "I take the métro to the end of the line to stroll in the Bois. Near a major thoroughfare I meet a traffic-jam whore. I stop to talk and find out she is actually a suburban housewife."

"Some wife!" snorted Susan.

"On summer weekends she takes a train into the city to perform tricks in the park. I ask her why. She tells me she enjoys the challenge of so many lovers in a short time."

"Hah!" exclaimed Susan. "The only thing she really enjoys is the pay! A woman might do anything for money."

"You've never said that before," said Jeff, a puzzled look crossing his face.

"Continue," urged Susan. "I want to hear more about your whore. You can't imagine how she interests me."

"Where did we stop before you interrupted?" Jeff asked.

"You had just mentioned that she had many lovers," said Susan.

"Oh, yes. She also earns more money during the afternoon jam than her husband can earn all week at the office."

"Does he work in Paris?" Susan asked.

"Of course," replied Jeff. "Everybody who is anybody in France works in Paris."

"Does he travel by car during rush hour?" asked Susan, amused by a sudden idea.

"You won't catch me that way!" laughed Jeff. "He takes another route. In fact, he suspects nothing and assumes she comes into the city on shopping sprees. The woman finances her family's vacation in Provence."

"Mostly she buys clothes and household luxuries," quipped Susan.

"I suppose she buys some of those things too," replied Jeff. "Her husband assumes the extra money comes from interest she receives from an inheritance. When I ask the woman about her business in the park, she says—"

Susan interrupted Jeff to complete his sentence. "The afternoon shift is definitely superior to the morning. Commuters have been in offices all day and are looking forward to getting home. They have a lot of unburned energy. When traffic ties up, they are quick to spend money for a few moments of ecstasy behind a bush or tree. I'm careful to choose men I desire, since there are always more than enough. I take them behind my own special tree, only a few meters from the road. The tree is broad enough to hide lovemaking from other drivers. Most men prefer intimacy."

"Do you man your post during the early morning rush?" Jeff inquired.

"What a silly question!" remarked Susan. "No, never. I have to fix my husband's breakfast. Also, mornings are difficult and the love itself is no fun. Commuters have just come from wives and don't need a girl. A few will pay, but their minds are on business. They lift skirts and screw hard. That's no good. It makes a girl physically sore and angry."

"That's horrible!" Jeff exclaimed, with real disgust in his voice.

"That's why I've never desired to be here in the morning," explained Susan. "Plus it's cold at that time of day. I'd have to wear a coat and bring along a thermos of hot coffee. That would be clumsy."

"Are you open for business now?" Jeff asked.

"Not really," Susan replied. "Rush hour won't begin for another hour. Right now I'm going to have a picnic lunch. Why do you ask?"

"You're really quite beautiful," said Jeff.

"Are you interested in me?" asked Susan coyly. She stood up and sidled along the shore. "If you've got cash, I suppose I could oblige you, though I'd rather not. Don't get me wrong. Physically you're okay, but I prefer to choose partners. I take only those of great appeal. Many men prefer me to the pros. I don't look used. I try to keep fresh, even at my age."

"It's okay," Jeff replied, hurt. "I don't mind if we refrain. It's too hot anyway." He pulled at his shirt and wiped accumulated brine from his forehead.

"Too hot?" Susan asked. "But this is Paris. It's a beautiful day. Birds are chirping and light is filtering through the trees. Why do you say that?"

"It's the type of love," said Jeff, whose voice quite suddenly became intense and nervous. "Jesus, Susan, you really do sound like a whore. And why did you say you'd rather not do it with me? Plus you make it sound like a line will soon follow—dozens of strange men! You really do!"

"Oh, it's not like that at all," Susan argued as she continued to play her role. Damnit, she thought. You're not going to get me back to reality now, not when things are just starting to get somewhere. "The loveplay is so frantic I hardly notice a change of customers. It's not much different from an hour of extended lovemaking with one partner. You for instance. Afterwards I find it marvelously invigorating." Susan walked over to where Jeff still sat and stood directly in front of him, her legs apart, her naked body outthrust, her hands wrapped in her long hair piled on top of her head.

"I don't understand," Jeff said. "All of this is strange."

"Why don't you join me for a bit to eat?" Susan asked. "I brought some wine and several kinds of pâté for the baguettes. I know nothing about you. Are you American?"

"Yes," Jeff said.

"Well, you must be *sportif*," laughed Susan, who hadn't used French for years and was proud she could remember the words. "Why don't you take a swim with me? It will give you an appetite."

Jeff reluctantly began to undress. He felt oddly shy in front of the naked Susan, as if he had never seen her before.

When they returned to the car, Jeff drove. He was in a talkative mood. The air had cooled considerably as the sun slid toward the horizon. There seemed to be less dust in the air, and for the first time Jeff noticed a muted beauty in the prairie scenery. "I feel great," he said, glancing fondly toward Susan. "That swim was just what I needed."

Susan said nothing. Feeling empty and alone, she slouched against the passenger door.

"The air is cooling fast now," Jeff continued. "It's going to be a lovely evening. Mademoiselle," he said, addressing Susan as if they were still playing the game, "I hope you serve the same delicious lunch next time. Under the same tree."

Susan, fidgeting, thrust bare feet onto the diminutive dash.

"We should have camped there a couple of days," said Jeff. "There was no reason why we had to leave."

"I didn't like the place, Jeff," snapped Susan. She felt burned out and exhausted. "We should get as far as possible before dark."

"What's gotten into you?" Jeff asked. "Why are you suddenly such a spoilsport?"

Susan could not reply. She glared out at the flat monotony which surrounded them. Her blouse was sticking uncomfortably to her back. Inside she felt very small, weak, and helpless. She squinted from grit in her eyes, but that wasn't why she wanted to cry. She stared over at Jeff, at his suddenly renewed enthusiasm. He was positively glowing as he guided their worn-out Volkswagen down a bleak, dusty road. He was acting like the captain of a ship heading for port with a precious cargo. Will anything ever happen? Susan wondered. She felt like an old crone who had outlived everything—family, friends, work. I am an Eve without an Adam or an Abel or a Cain or a God, she realized. Nothingness was imprinted on her soul as if in indelible black ink.

"Will we ever grow up?" she asked Jeff. In the empty silence she waited for his reply.